THE FINAL
VICTIM

By: Larry Jukofsky

Published by Graveyard Publishing

Vine Grove, KY U.S.A.

© 2010 Graveyard Publishing

Published by arrangement with the author.

First Graveyard Printing September 2010

Distributed by Graveyard Publishing

200 Redbird Ct. Vine Grove, KY 40175 U.S.A.

http://www.graveyardpublishing.com/

ISBN: 978-0-578-06967-8

To contact the author, forward all correspondence to Graveyard Publishing at the above address, or email to: graveyard@graveyardpublishing.com Please out the Authors name in the subject line, and we will forward your correspondence to the Author

This book is dedicated to my girls, Betsy and Diane.

My blessings and thanks to my wife Betsy and my daughter Diane for first reading this over and correcting so much and to Scott, my favorite editor for everything else; except for all I learned from Bram Stoker and Bela Lugosi.

~THE FINAL VICTIM~

PROLOGUE

They had been in transport for four hours. The freight car was filled with men, women, and children so tightly packed that no one could sit. He recalled reading, many years ago about something described as "The Black Hole of Calcutta." Intermittently those affected with claustrophobia screamed and cursed. Women and children were crying. The only light in the car was that which came through small cracks in the sides of the car. There was the smell of vomit and urine everywhere. He'd seen his parents shot in front of their home, and his three sisters carried off in a truck with other girls. This was not a good time to be alive. He wondered what kind of work they would have to do for them. Either that or they would be killed. He prayed silently.

The train stopped suddenly and caused the occupants of the car to fall forward against each other. There was no room to actually fall down. The door to the side slid open and light poured in hurting his eyes. A soldier ordered everyone out of the car. In their eagerness to get out, many fell to the ground on exiting. Looking about, he saw what seemed to be hundreds of uniformed soldiers carrying rifles and pistols. One officer carried a loudspeaker and lined up everyone. They were told that they were to. shower before entering the camp and going into the barracks. All clothes must be removed including shoes and left in a pile to the sides of the lines. Intermittent gunfire sounded in the distance intermittent. Fear conquered the lines of people.

Fear conquered embarrassment. They were marched to a large garage like building with the word *"schauer"* printed on a large sign on the front and herded inside. The crowding inside the building was not as intense as it was in the freight-car, but there was little room between the naked bodies. He glanced up at the ceiling and saw no nozzles or shower-heads. Only a few pipes crossed the area. There were holes in those pipes. He did not expect that the water would be heated. No soap was provided yet. The doors slid shut and the room darkened. They waited silently now for the shower to start. There was no crying except for a few of the children, and no one was cursing as they had in the freight car.

A hissing sound from above made him look up. He realized now what was happening. The gas had a smell he had never encountered before. The occupants of the site began coughing and screaming, losing control of urine and feces. He felt sudden nausea.

"This is my reward for faith and love of you God?" He shouted at the pipes above. "What kind of God does this to his followers? I hate you! I curse you! Damn you and your teachings! I will revenge myself for this! Go to hell, God!" He inhaled deeply several times and died.

~THE FINAL VICTIM~

"Son of a bitch!" muttered Rudy Singleton as he drove through the heavy downpour. The Sunbelt had come out of a drought period suddenly. His windshield wipers were not clearing his view rapidly enough for decent visibility. Rudy made his living doing odd jobs on the island and picking up freight of all sorts with his pick-up truck and delivering it from the airport and other sites on the mainland to the island. Breakers View Island depended on trucking for all goods as there was no rail connection, and its airport was too small for large planes. In addition to the visibility problems, he had gastric and headache difficulties to contend with at the moment. As usual, Rudy had overeaten lunch. His pants never reached the gluteal region of his body due to the presence of a potbelly. This was most evident when Rudy stooped over to lift things. He had a full beard having not shaved in a year. His hair hung down the back of his neck and well over his ears, since he had also not had a professional cut in over a year. The jeans he wore all the time were too small to cover his overweight body. The pickup truck was filled with smoke and had the odor of onions and tobacco at all times. The ashtrays had never been emptied and had spilled their contents over the dashboard area. In appearance, Rudy was overall unacceptable in society, which mattered little to the man.

He stopped the truck at the overpass hoping the rain would ease up. He lit a cigarette, waited for fifteen minutes, and then started driving toward the island again with the freight he'd picked up at the airport.

er thought I'd be driving a hearse for a livin'!" he said ./onder who the poor bastard is in there!"

Rudy had no family he knew about. His friends lived lives similar to his in dress and appearance, and were few in number and usually frequented the bars he visited for contacts. He rarely sought the company of women. His meager income came from jobs such as this and from assisting in the removal of refuse from island hotels and homes. He'd come out of the orphanage at the age of seventeen and had not bettered his lifestyle in the six years since. He also added to his income by parking near the taxi stand at the airport and carrying the extra luggage that would not fit into the individual taxi. His female companions consisted of occasional prostitutes.

For some reason, Rudy was uncomfortable tonight, physically and mentally. Transporting a coffin was a new experience. It frightened him. Superstition played a large role in his limited educational life. Here it was dark, stormy, and he was delivering a corpse. The route took him through wooded and desolate country, with hanging Spanish moss casting eerie shadows as he drove by. His bright lights were on, only being dimmed when a car came from the opposite direction. The lighting and thunder added to the unease caused by the downpour. Rudy's grasp of the steering wheel was quite tight. The rhythmical beat of the windshield wiper was his only entertainment as the radio had not worked in quite some time. Rudy was horrified when a bolt of lightning seemed to strike the ground quite close to his truck. It took considerable effort to hold the wheel firmly. Through the rear view mirror he could so no flames and concluded no damage had been done to his cargo. The dead guy in back wouldn't mind a jolt or two anyhow, would he?

Thinking the better of his decision to continue driving in this downpour, he pulled over to the side of the highway. It was when he turned off the motor that he realized he was not alone in the truck. He had a passenger seated alongside him.

At six in the evening, Murray LaVine met with Rabbi Ira Silman. Murray was president of the Temple Bethel congregation on Breakers View Island. He and his wife lived in a plantation next to the temple location. On the island, what were called "housing developments" elsewhere in the country were called plantations. These were abundant in the Sunbelt States. They were gated communities supported in maintenance by resident assessments with no outside controls. About seven or eight of these made up much of the island. Breakers View Island had a population about thirty thousand, half of whom lived behind gates.

Murray LaVine was about five feet, six inches in height and balding. He'd had a head of red hair at the earlier stages of his life. At sixty-nine, he exhibited a large abdominal bulge in addition to the sparse hair and had a chubby face. On a resort island where most men were dressed informally, Murray always wore a necktie and jacket

"Something must have happened at the airport. Plane was probably late with the rain and all. Bad weather probably held him up." he addressed the congregation's spiritual leader. They sat in the rabbi's study, which was a small room in the rear of the temple. It had a desk, three folding chairs, and a small book case.

Rabbi Ira Silman had moved to the island two years previously and had established firm roots. He had seen his congregation grow from a scant forty members to over two hundred in that time. He was about the same height as the president of the temple but had a full head of groomed black, curly hair, and a small mustache of the same color. It made him appear older than his thirty-six years. He dressed in a more

anner than LaVine, wearing slacks, an open shirt, and
vith no socks.

/be we should phone the airport." The rabbi picked up
ne to dial. "Forget it. No dial tone at present. Storm!"
Loss of the use of the phone was common on the island after
heavy weather.

"Happens often here! Freak storm! Haven't seen a
thunderstorm like this one in quite a while. Nothing about it on
the radio." There was only the one local radio broadcasting
station, but several other stations were received from the
mainland.

"Glad I got Moe to put a tarp over that hole. We'd a had a
swimming pool instead of a gravesite shrine with this much
rain."

"That is a cleaver decision on the part of the committee,
Murray. It'll be beneficial to the temple. Give people something
to think about and remember. After seventy, eighty years, the
world forgets about the horrors these people endured."

"I got the idea when I read about them discovering a mass
grave at a housing development site. Can you imagine digging
for foundations and finding skeletons?"

"It must have horrified the workmen. I heard it on the news.
No pictures though. Good idea not to show any. So the shrine
will be dedicated to the memory of Holocaust victims. But we
only have one of the victims."

Murray beamed at the reference to his idea. What a good way
to bring publicity to the temple! A shrine dedicated to victims of
the holocaust. He'd read about the discovery in Poland. A great
way to increase membership!

"I suppose the goyem will think we are raising money
somehow. Like charging a fee to view the shrine. I will write a
letter to the editor stating that this is not so! The public should be

[10]

informed of what we went through to get permission for this. To get the remains sent here. Thank God for the senator's help. What red tape! Unbelievable! So many letters! Back and forth! Washington! And Poland!"

"Listen! It was worse with Europe! I can't tell you how many calls Hedva had to make. You'd think we were asking for gold relics."

"Well, the worst part is over. Finally it's here. Looks like the trip from the airport is gonna be longer than the trip to the states."

"Rain like this! At least we know it's here."

"Yeah! Another day or so.!"

"Treblinka must have been hell on earth! Who is going to move into a home on top of a mass gravesite? Gotta be real desperate for a house."

"It was only a hundred miles from Warsaw. Mastonowicz! Town created after the war. Fifty or more skeletons in one grave. My God! What a smell! And to think there would be one perfectly preserved corpse in all that. The letter says that once in a while the gas had an embalming effect on the bodies. Good thing they put ours into refrigeration right away. Filled the casket with dirt too or we would have had quite a smell here too."

"Poland tried to keep the thing quiet, but word got out anyway."

"Damn phones are still dead. That's the trouble with living on an island. Bet the mainland isn't having any difficulties."

"Probably lightning knocked out the line."

The following morning was a hectic one for Murray LaVine. He spent an hour on the phone at his home and another on the phone at the temple. The airport knew nothing related to the whereabouts of Rudy Singleton or his cargo. The police knew

[11]

nothing about any accidents on the road to the island. The groundskeeper at the temple was no help.

"Suh! I been here all mornin'. Didn't leave until about eleven last night. Nobody and nothin' came by truck or anythin' else."

Moe Pinckney was an elderly Black whose family had lived on the island for several generations. His ancestors went back to pre-Civil War days. He was a thin man with graying, sparse hair. Moe always seemed to have an unlit half cigar in his mouth. And it never even came out of that site, even when he spoke. He wore jeans and a white shirt that needed ironing. His hat was a dirty pith helmet, which had become an island-wide recognized symbol for the man.

"Well shit, Moe! Nobody seems to know where the hell Singleton is and where his truck has disappeared to. Nobody loses a coffin! He picked it right up at the airport yesterday. During the heavy rain. Shoulda been here with it last night! Where the hell is he and that damn truck of his?"

"Mebbe he got stalled in the rain. Engine got too wet or somethin'."

"Maybe he stopped at a bar too. Damn it!" Murray went inside the temple and called the rabbi at his home to tell him what had happened.

"I think you should call the police. Don't waste time Murray!"

"First I'm gonna call that trailer camp where he lives. See if he came in. If there is no phone there I'll send the police out. They'll think I'm crazy. Losing a casket!"

"We gotta act fast. I'll be right over."

"Yes this is Murray LaVine. I am the president of Temple Bethel on Breakers View. We seem to have lost something. You won't believe me at first." He explained what had happened to the policeman on the line.

[12]

"We'll see what we can find out sir, and call you back. I'll send a deputy out there to see what's what. Call you back. Never had a missing casket before."

"I'd appreciate it."

"This is Tony Picket at post three. I read about a coffin being shipped out there. Why anybody might steal one I don't know. I'll have the men check the road to the island. Might have gone off in the rain."

As soon as Murray hung up, the phone rang. The rabbi was calling. "Nobody at the trailer camp has seen anything of the truck or Rudy for two days now."

"Damn it! We've got publicity comin' here for a story on our plans this afternoon. T.V. guy too!"

"Better call off the interview for now, Murray. It'll make for a better interview when we find the thing."

"Rudy may be layin' in some ditch with a hangover. He must have some kind of insurance or they wouldn't let him pick up stuff at the airport."

LaVine went outside the temple to the rear of the building where Moe was raking the area around the open pit that was to have held the coffin, the gravesite of a holocaust victim.

"Someone comes around asking questions, you know nothing, Moe."

"You got that right, sir. Know nothin' and don't want to know anythin'!"

"Better hang around case Rudy shows up. You got to tell him where we want that thing to go."

A patrol car pulled up in front of the temple and Tony Pickett got out and introduced himself to the president.

"So what's happening, Mister Pickett?"

"I have a crew checking the highway from the airport to here. So far nothing." Pickett was a short chubby man, with an Irish face and a full head of red hair. He had a turned up pug nose and a wide waistline and appeared to be in top physical condition. The muscular power and physical development was quite obvious. He was forty-eight and had been with the police force in this area for six years. He'd left a position with the Tulsa, Oklahoma police because of domestic problems with an alcoholic wife. He was dressed in a sport shirt and slacks at the moment. He usually wore a dark jacket with matching slacks, but never a necktie. Pickett headed the county detective section and had a staff of five to six deputies. In addition to this section of the constabulary, there was a county highway patrol. Pickett lived alone in a small house near the county seat. He did not socialize and had an excellent record at his job. The island and the county fathers considered themselves lucky to have him in charge.

"I'll see what I can find out and get back to you, sir." He took the temple number down and drove off."

"I know Tony! He don't find it, it ain't findable!" said Moe.

"Oh, we'll find the damn thing. Things like that don't disappear into thin air. Why would anyone want a pine box with a body in it? Can't have any value to anybody."

"Folks do a lot of crazy things these days. This is the craziest I ever heard of." Moe returned to the rear of the temple and continued raking the gravesite area. Murray returned to his home.

Pickett sat by his phone and office radio all morning at the station house. He kept in contact with his searching staff. He was quite sympathetic with the island Jewish population, which had been such a minority for so long now. Building the temple had changed things for them. They had gathered at the Methodist Church on Friday nights and Saturday mornings until the temple was built. Pickett recalled the anti-Semitic feelings he had to deal with before then. He worried that this occurrence would bring back some of that feeling again. There were some

[14]

organized groups that he'd dealt with before and hop/
not have to deal with again. There were Black fract
caused some troubles along those lines in earlier day﹅ .
the stirring up by the media starting with difficulties in New
York, which had led to some rioting there and carried to some
areas of the South.

Deputy Archie Hay drove the route taken by Singleton from
the airport for the third time. Starting from the pickup point at
the airport, he drove slowly, stopping at several sites to inspect
the terrain in case the truck had gone off the road. The growth
along the roadside was high in some areas and he wanted to
check for suspicious areas of damaged brush or bushes. A few
miles before the causeway to the island he noticed what appeared
to be a mowed down section of brush. An abandoned fire tower
stood several hundred feet behind the site. He directed the
spotlight on his vehicle towards the disturbed area and got out of
the vehicle with his flashlight and walked into the growing
weeds along the side of the parked car.

"Hello! Anybody here?" he called out. "Singleton!" there was
no response and he walked in further. "Singleton!" Still no
response. He was covered by insects now and swatted at the
cluster around his head, shutting off the attracting beam of his
flashlight. Hay wondered how people had lived in this area years
ago without bug spray or screened windows. He supposed they
got used to the atmosphere of the place after a time. Whoever the
guy was that had to man that fire tower must have been
uncomfortable all the time. Probably one of those Blacks that
spoke Gullah. Never did understand that talk. He walked into the
wooded area away from the road now. The site was surrounded
by massive oak trees, pine trees, and weeded growth taller than
he. Damn Singleton, he thought, swatting at bugs. He turned to
return to his car and turned his flashlight back on and saw the

vehicle. It was backed into a growth of weeds, vines, and covered with leaves. Archie put on his gloves and brushed away the growth from the truck. It was empty as far as he could see, and fit the description of the vehicle for which he was searching. Pulling his cell phone from his jacket, he called headquarters and was advised to stay with the vehicle and to put the lights on his car on for backup to follow. Returning to the truck, he noticed it had gotten to this location without mowing down weeds. It was as if it had been picked up and placed there.

In forty minutes there were three county vehicles joining Hay's, plus a tow truck. The area was searched for several hundred yards around the truck but there was no sign of Rudy anywhere, nor was there any cargo in the back of the truck. The far edge of this area of growth was bordered by the John Tompkins Creek. It was actually not a creek, but a river; the name given to it after the Civil War. Nobody had ever bothered to stop calling it a creek however and the name persisted. A mile or two away it ran into the ocean. The truck was photographed from all angles the next morning and the area searched more intensively. Nothing else was found, so the truck was towed to the county yard to be examined for whatever else could be discovered.

The back of the vehicle revealed scrape marks that indicated a large object had been dragged off. It still held half a tank of gasoline, and the glove compartment was empty. Some life was still in the battery. All clues indicated that the truck had probably been hijacked, the cargo stolen, and the driver kidnapped and possibly slain.

That was the wrong conclusion. On the back waters of this undeveloped land area were many wrecks of boats that had been used for fishing. Some had been there for over two hundred years, slowly rotting away. They had been used for shrimping, which was, and still is, an important industry in the area. Smaller wrecks had been used for transport and fishing for lesser cargo. Most, when ready for disposal, had been towed out into the ocean and scuttled. But many were just abandoned to the elements. How some of these wrecks got to be so far from the ocean shore was a mystery. The rivers must have been more navigable in the past was one explanation.

Such a wreck was the "Delilah." It laid leaning to its port side about eight miles inland, in a swampy area of John Tompkins Creek. This was about four miles from where the Singleton truck had been found. The history of the craft was unknown. The state had many of these wrecks in it, particularly in the section known as "The Low Country." Breakers View Island was in that geographical location. The name on the abandoned vessel was still discernable. The area was full of swampy growth and mud. The insect population created a symphonic-like chorus at night, and only stopped when sounds were made that were not native to the area. There were some sounds coming from the abandoned wreck now. It was occupied.

The hull had been cleared of weeds and other growth, mud, and debris. Three wooden crates had been aligned in a row to create a foundation for a large coffin bearing a six-pointed star painted on the cover centrally. There were no porthole openings in this area of the wreck as this had been the site of the motor that had propelled this shrimp boat in earlier days. On the far side of this space were two more crates placed together to form a platform of sorts on which lay the sleeping figure of Rudy Singleton. On close inspection one would see that his eyes were opened and fixed as if he were in some kind of trance. His clothing, now muddy and damp, was what he'd worn when he picked up his cargo at the airport.

Getting the coffin from the parked truck to the Delilah had not been a difficult task due to the amazing strength of his helper. That individual had dispatched Rudy to get the crates from the rear of a supermarket on the island. The truck had been abandoned far from the wreck and covered with weeds to hide it. The river was actually unapproachable from this or the other side.

Rudy arose the morning of the day the truck was discovered by Archie Hay and walked for about an hour to the highway. On reaching that point, he waited until a garbage truck passed and stopped it. He was told to ride in the back because he smelled and was covered with filth from the swamp. On arriving at the island, he jumped from the truck and hid in the rear of a supermarket until it opened for business at nine. He entered the store and began stuffing fruit into his pocket, was apprehended and held for the police. He was then arrested for shoplifting. He was identified and held for questioning by Tony Pickett.

"Can't make out what in the hell he's sayin'!" Bill Boyd complained to his superior, Archie Hay. Archie was senior deputy under Tony Pickett on the force. Born on Breakers View Island, he had lived there most of his life. With tutoring by his superior, Tony, he managed to pass the necessary tests to achieve his present status on the detective force. This was difficult for a high school dropout. He was tall, over six feet two inches and well developed with muscles as a result of exercising with barbells. He had a crooked nose, having had it broken after receiving blows to it several times in his career. His blond hair was long and ended well below his neckline. Archie had a black belt in karate and used that ability in his line of work many times. He'd never been married and lived with another deputy in a small house near the entrance to the island approach causeway. His sex life was full and varied and he was a popular man with the age group in which he socialized.

The cell block ran down the far side of the headquarters building. There were seven cells but only one was occupied, this by Rudy Singleton. The cells had a cot and a sink plus a commode with no seat. The cells were basically holding units until the occupant was transferred to the county jail on the mainland. Across from the line of cells was the door to the office of the unit, which held Tony Pickett's desk and the file cabinets of the force. Another small desk was used by the members of the force to write up their reports. It was on the side of the main desk. On the other side of the room were cabinets holding rifles and other supplies. There were two windows in this room. The cells had tiny windows high on the back walls of each.

"Let's see what I can do," said Archie.

"Yeah! Let's see how an expert does it!"

"Jus' watch and learn, Billy boy!"

Tony Pickett entered the cell area at this moment. "What's up?"

"Boyd can't get Singleton to say anything or can't get him to say anything he understands."

"Go ahead Arch. I'll watch!"

Singleton sat stiffly on the cot in his cell staring at the opposite wall. Picket noticed dilated pupils and the fact the man did not seem to blink. Drugs? He'd had Rudy's clothes removed and the man now wore the orange jumpsuit prison attire. He'd been put in the shower to remove the mud and filth, and he now wore scuff slippers instead of his thoroughly soaked with mud and silt shoes and socks.

"How's it goin', Rudy?"

There was no acknowledgement of Archie's question.

"You hear what I'm sayin' boy?"

"He talk any when you brought him in?" asked Tony.

"He was saying somethin' but it made no sense."

"Let me give it a try." Tony unlocked the door to the cell and entered. He sat on the cot alongside Rudy. "Can you hear me son?"

[19]

"I sure can." Rudy turned his head towards Tony.

"Then tell us where you been?"

"*Mit Karen meister.*"

"And who's that?"

"My teacher. He teaches me."

"Where is your teacher now?"

"*Kasette!*"

"Cassette? On tape?"

"Sleeping comfortable."

"He sleeps on a cassette? On a tape recorder?"

"*Karen meister*. Tells me what to do."

"Cow and master who?"

"I care for."

"All!"

"All what?"

"Not to say!"

For the next fifteen minutes they could not get Rudy to say anything else. It was as though he had suddenly been told to shut up.

"Damn! Wish we had recorded this."

"I wrote it all down Tony! Somethin' about his master and a cow, and I guess a tape recorder."

"We better get this guy to the county. Needs a loony bin. We'll get in trouble if we keep him here."

"Sure sounds like a nut to me."

Rudy was taken out to a squad car and placed in the rear caged seat. There was no access to door handles in that spot. A screen separated the passengers in the rear from the driver in front. It took about fifteen minutes to drive to the county jail on the mainland. No one spoke during the drive. On arrival Tony handed over the prisoner and the paperwork.

Rudy was placed in a security ward for observation. A psychiatrist would be in the next morning to question the man.

[20]

Rudy no longer responded to questioning. Recorders were placed to take down anything that came out of his cell now. During the night, Rudy made some sounds that sounded like a code language of some sort. He defecated sitting on the toilet but lifted his leg to urinate against the cot. He refused to eat anything on the tray placed in his cell except a small portion of the meat. He drank water, but no other beverage given to him. At midnight he got off the cot and paced back and forth in his cell like an animal in a cage. The attendant decided that this was a real nut case and did not try to communicate with Rudy the rest of the night.

A doctor took over the next morning and spent most of the day with Rudy. The final conclusion, after x-rays and lab work and three more days of questioning was that this was a healthy, semi-insane individual with a personality shift toward that of a carnivorous animal.

It had rained heavily. Karl Licht, the owner of the Baden Baden Restaurant, placed the "closed" sign inside the entrance door window. Business had been good that evening. In seventy years he had never been so financially independent. The name of the establishment had been derived from a German spa noted for its mineral waters and health treatments. The money to establish the restaurant had been spirited out of Argentina once he had obtained the visas for himself and his family. That had been accomplished by a multitude of bribes using finances obtained from the restaurant he'd established in La Plata.

He gathered the receipts from the night's business and went back to the small office behind the dining area. He arranged the bills so that they were stacked under papers with listed headings. These headings were named after the various destinations for the sums placed there. Some were charities that elected the needy publicity for his business. He wanted the name "Licht" to be associated with charitable giving on Breakers View Island. It

[21]

was essential to get the public's respect in this manner to prevent research into his past. Licht led parades, appeared on television programs, donating to whatever fund was featured at the time. He was a member of local service clubs, volunteered to work on whatever project was current, and went out of his way to become a known and popular figure. His wife, on the other hand did not appear in the public eye, and his two children lived elsewhere. Licht's son and daughter hated their father. When they did get together as a family, the son-in-law belittled the man constantly. His son barely spoke with his father. His daughter's children avoided him altogether and rarely came to the island with their parents.

He managed to live with the family situation. The important thing was that there was no tracing back to his life in Europe. It would mean disaster if the facts of that previous life were made known to the public. His wife Anna was more of a maid-servant than a companion in marriage. She too lived in fear of exposure.

The Baden Baden had opened at four in the afternoon. Karl was the first to arrive. The waiters and waitresses, the chief and kitchen help arrived about fifteen minutes later. There had been heavy reservations made for the evening. The front desk receptionist scanned the listings and reported the important names to the maitre d'hôtel.

"Gonna be busy, Mister Licht," announced the head waiter.

"Good! Good! Get the early ones in and out as fast as you can. Tell the staff to get the desert order at the same time as the entrée. That gets them through faster. Nobody waits until the bill is requested. Bring it with the coffee. If they get upset tell them you didn't think they'd want after dinner brandy or whatever. That'll sell some."

Licht had worked hard in Argentina at changing his German accent to something unidentifiable. He had one now that could not be associated with any particular origin. At his desk in the rear office he now sat and thought about the past. There were years of evasion after "forty-six". He recalled the days in Hamburg, his birthplace. Days there had been terrible. National Socialists appealed to him then. He'd been an adjutant of Heydrich for a time and had been involved in the horrors that history revealed later. Licht anticipated the retribution that would follow and never allowed photographs of the era to include him. His name was rarely mentioned in any official document of the era. As he sat at his desk he smiled at his intelligence in realizing that Hitler and his tactics were doomed to failure, and that history would take revenge on all those involved. He had planned for the post-Nazi failure at a time when it often was most successful, and sent large sums of money to Argentina where he went as soon as he could with his family. He had no guilt feelings about the fact that the moneys had been obtained from slaughtered Jewish families. Israel's attention to the German refugees in Argentina forced his attention to the obtaining of American visas sooner than he planned.

Karl entered the previous day's receipts in his ledger. He routinely kept cash payments in a separate ledger from the credit and check income. Licht reasoned that his was not the only business that did this kind of record keeping. His method of "laundering money" was to write a large salary check to himself and to pocket the unrecorded cash as well.

His children knew about his past. They lived as far away as they could from their parents without avoiding their mother. Anna Licht was happy that they had moved away. They thought that they might be exposed was something she dreaded. She was aware of the hidden mementos in their attic. Some of these things nauseated her but she never mentioned that box to anyone, not even her children. Karl knew she would never expose that secret cache. Time had erased her conscience and she continued to live under the same roof with the man that she hated.

It was after midnight when Karl finished working on the books in his office. The rest of the staff had departed after cleaning up the tables and the kitchen. The chairs were stacked on the tables to make cleaning the floor easier. He sat back and reflected on how things were going so well for him. Anna was a bit of a problem but could be handled easily and kept subdued. The children wanted nothing to do with him, needed no financial support, and kept a satisfying distance. Good riddance!

He put on the jacket that had been draped over the desk chair. He intended to sleep until noon the next day. Anna wouldn't bother him. He hadn't approached her sexually for so long that he couldn't recall the last endeavor. Looking at himself in the full length mirror behind his desk, he saw a tall man with a typical, haughty, Prussian appearance. It was an erect individual, with a crew cut head that denoted superiority. He was somewhat stout, but with a commanding air of self-satisfaction. He felt quite satisfied with his physical condition for his age.

He turned out the lights and went into the dining area. There was no light from the moon that night and it took him time to get his eyes adapted to the dark. Intermittent lights went through the room from passing cars. It was very quiet. Karl was startled when he realized that he was not alone in the large room. He knew the front door of the restaurant was locked. A figure stood by the door, inside, and outlined by the passing lights of cars.

"Who's there? How did you get in here?" Karl was more startled than frightened.

The figure did not move, but he eyes seemed to glow. It reminded Karl of a pumpkin with a candle glowing from within the cut out eye area. He backed up to his office door. This must be a robber he thought.

"Stop right there. I have access to an alarm system here."

The figure advanced toward Karl. Combat training from the old days made him sure he could handle this robber and he tensed for attack. The eyes caught his attention, and as he looked at the two glowing sites a feeling of weakness came over him. He dropped the cash box that he held under his arm. The figure moved quickly up close to Karl and spoke with a deep, hoarse, inhuman voice. "Treblinka!"

A hand with an iron grip shot out and literally lifted Karl off his feet, grabbing him by the shoulder. The other hand reached out and tore off the front of Karl's neck. He then dropped the body onto the floor.

Most restaurants that do not serve lunch are closed until late afternoon. Ancillary help arrives at that time to get the place ready for the evening business. Sheila Carson unlocked the entrance door at the Baden Baden and entered the eatery. She went right to her desk at the doorway and sat in her chair behind the high slanted top of the desk. It would be forty-five minutes before the rest of the help arrived. She usually put the books in order and laid out the table assignments. Her employer would then check the books before she made any entrees. The first diners would be served at six-forty. These would be the "early-bird" specials usually served to an elderly crowd. It was important to get the servers to get these customers out by eight to make room for the diners who were considered more lucrative. The early diners were mostly retirees. That group had been the earliest settlers on the island. They wanted services, which led to the growth of a younger age group. These were the waiters, gas station attendants, and other people like them. This group turned out to be more fertile which led to the necessity for more schools, which led to resentment by the retirees who had already been taxed to build schools before settling there. The necessity for housing the service population also led to resentment of the sudden building surge. Business interests resented the opposition to development that ensued. The business interests won out, and the island tourist trade grew. More and more young people were needed to care for the increasing tourist population and so a cycle of development began that led to isolation of retirees into gated communities. Property taxes increased as did traffic.

Sheila Carson was in her late twenties. Before being hired by Karl Licht, she had been a movie theatre usherette. With brown hair, a turned-up nose, and a figure that produced admiring stares by customers. She was given the position of greeting-hostess. She was driven to work each day by her husband (an island taxi driver) who then picked her up at night. After getting her desk ready, Sheila walked over and checked the burglar alarm. This was usually turned off by her employer earlier in the afternoon and on before he left at about midnight. He was usually last to leave. She signed the employee sheet at the desk to the left of hers. It indicated time of arrival of employees. She put on a jacket furnished by her employer, glanced at her hairdo in a mirror by the door, sat down on the chair at her station and inspected the reservation list. The chairs were still stacked on the tables. The rest of the staff would place them on the floor at the tables when they arrived. She really did not like this job but it paid well. Her husband had to eat alone every night. And she wished they could afford a second car so that he wouldn't have to pick her up every night. It kept him from his work, which could be lucrative in the late hours. She placed her feet on the fluffy mat under her desk for comfort. Licht had decided to leave the linoleum flooring that had come with the restaurant that preceded the Baden Baden in this location. It had been a singles bar and grill and the flooring seemed to match the décor that Licht had installed, so it was not changed. She glanced at the bar and noticed that the stool at the far left was missing and went over to see where it had been misplaced.

[26]

"Mister Licht! Are you alright?" The inert figure lay on the floor to the left of the bar. It was face down. She recognized the white sweater with the edelweiss he usually wore to go home at the end of the workday, and shook his shoulder. There was no response. "You drink too much or somethin'?" Still no response. This had happened before. He usually passed out at his desk though. She tried to roll him over on his back and got a glimpse of the neck area. It was avulsed with a six or seven inch gap with blood lining the edges of the area. She screamed and ran to her desk and dialed nine-one-one.

The patrol car was there in seven minutes. Sheila had turned on all the lights, including the outside sign lights, and then returned to her desk and promptly fainted. When the police arrived and entered they found her on the floor by her desk, revived her, and asked her what the problem was. She said nothing but pointed at the bar.

Two more police cars were there within ten minutes. The room filled with police, department photographers, and people from the emergency squad and ambulance. A coroner's representative declared the corpse officially dead and it was removed after being thoroughly examined and photographed to the ambulance, which left for the county morgue. Tony Pickett was assigned the case for investigation. With all the people in the room, he decided that a check for fingerprints would be useless. Archie Hay had placed yellow strips at the entrance denoting a crime scene. This arouses the curiosity of passersby and a crowd assembled outside. Arriving waters and kitchen help were turned away. Sheila's husband had been summoned and he arrived to take her home after she'd been thoroughly questioned by Pickett. Anna Licht had been notified. Questioned later by Archie Hay at her home, she stated that her husband's not returning last night had not alarmed her since he often did not come home at night after work. She assumed he was philandering again as he often did. She really did not like her husband much, and was pleased when he did not turn to her for anything. He had been a womanizer in Argentina and also back in Germany. When notified of the turn of events here, her children were also pleased.

When they were the only ones left at the scene, Tony and Archie walked about the restaurant.

"Notice anything, Arch?" They stood at the site where Licht's body had been found.

"Nothin' that tells me anythin'."

"Sure you don't see something?"

"Just the chalk outline. Don't see anythin' else!"

"That's right, Arch."

"What's right?"

"You don't see anything else."

"I ain't followin' you , sir."

"What's missing? Only thing we removed is the body."

"Yeah! Right, sir."

"And the hole in his neck is big enough to put a fist in, wasn't it? It was big enough of a gash to almost take the head off. Where is all the blood?"

"Yea! Jesus! It can't be."

"None anyplace except some on the body!"

"How can that be?"

"Didn't find any blood anyplace else. With him face down, should have been blood all over the floor, Arch!"

"Somebody done a big clean up here."

"So, it's possible that he got the gash elsewhere and he was dumped here. Sill I expected some blood on the floor or around here, Drops showing he was carried here. A trail or something."

"Seems he was so anemic he didn't bleed much!"

"Not possible. Even anemics bleed. Won't be many tracks outside after the heavy rain but we better look. Only two doors and an emergency exit. All locked! No keys missing. She said she didn't unlock anything but the front door and she is the only help with a key. Burglar alarm turned off. Now, if the boss had done that, he done it last night, and if he done it last night it wasn't ever turned on again."

"So somebody gets in without a key, turns off the alarm if Licht has it on. Kills Licht and locks the door without a key somehow behind him after wiping up a bloody mess."

"Looks that way."

"Jerry says when he called her; the wife didn't sound too unhappy."

"Go see her at home, Archie."

They checked the whole area once again. The deadbolts in the doors not unlocked by the girl were still closed. The evening's cash receipts were in a small bag under the owner's desk in the back office. His wallet was in his pocket and he was wearing a Rolex watch. Robbery had not been the motive for this killing.

"He must have fooled around with that gal. She's a looker."

"Can't see her involved in this. Husband picks her up at night and how is she gonna get the mess cleaned up?"

"Hires somebody to do the cleanin' or mebbe the husband helps her. Comes back after."

"Bags full of money left behind. Guard at the gate of their plantation says they didn't go back out after one. And the clean up was a good long job. No rug, but no linoleum around the bar. Wood flooring there. No blood even in the cracks between the wood pieces. And no robbery."

"See a lot of interviews ahead of us. Them two. And the waiters and kitchen people. Even some of the diners last night. And the Licht family."

[29]

A deputy called from the door. "Hey, Chief. Come lookee here!"

He pointed to three of the many prints around the wet steps and on them. There were three entrance steps made of wood at the front door. He pointed to the bottom step and to the muddy area by the left side of the steps.

"That's amazing!" exclaimed Archie Hay. "Them prints were made by the biggest dog I can imagine. Biggest I ever seen. Will, make casts of the ones in the mud. Get better shots of the ones on the steps."

José White, pathologist at the island hospital, was doing the autopsy in place of the county coroner who was on vacation. Pickett drove to the hospital to get the report from Doctor White, whose office was on the third floor of the hospital. He had to read an old Time magazine in the waiting room of the pathology lab until Jose arrived.

"Heard you were waiting. Got here as fast as I could."

"What you got for me, Doc?"

They were long standing friends. Both had arrived on the island at the same time. José White had not planned on making this a permanent career site, but the rapid development of the island had altered his long term plans. The new hospital had attracted doctors, causing an influx of medical activity. His wife Pam had connected with the elementary school as a teacher. The enrollment had tripled since her arrival on the island. She was settled in as the third grade teacher at various times, shifting each semester. The island became their permanent home sooner than they expected or intended.

White's desk was a disorderly mess of papers, books, and pathology slides. On the shelves behind the desk were more slides and bottles with specimens. A computer was on the right side on a small table. To the right of that was a small bookcase

[30]

with about twenty books. The one window in the room, on the right side, gave a view of the hospital roof. José wore an operating room uniform of green pants and a matching pullover shirt. An untied mask hung around his neck.

José White had been born and raised in Puerto Rico. The family had moved to Chicago when he was fourteen. His father was a Petty Officer in the U. S. Navy, and his mother was a registered nurse and worked in Chicago in a hospital. Her income from that and her husband's pension (he had been killed at Pearl Harbor) enabled José to get through medical school after finishing the University of Chicago, where he'd had a four year scholarship. His post graduate training had been in Italy. He was thin, tall, and muscular; kept there by a regime of intense and regular exercises. He had dark wavy hair, and a deep olive skin coloring.

"Let's go down to the morgue and I can show you what I found better than I can describe it."

Tony was not crazy about the morgue. He'd witnessed six or seven autopsies and had not enjoyed any of them. The formaldehyde smell of the place bothered him. They descended to the morgue located in the basement of the hospital on an elevator. Outside the morgue was a ramp leading to the building. Bodies were unloaded from the ambulance to gurneys and wheeled to one of three tables there. Five refrigerators for bodies were located behind the tables. There was a ceiling light over each table. Before this facility had been built, all bodies for pathological exams had been sent to the mainland morgue in the county coroner's office. This morgue had grown with the island.

José White pulled back the sheet that covered Karl Licht's body. Tony had put on a gown similar to that worn by José, with the same green mask. At first he stared at the tag on the big toe of the corpse and gradually brought his eyes up to the head.

[31]

"Pretty ugly, Tony. Haven't seen one like this since I got here."

Neither have I, thought Tony. Here or any place I have been before.

"Severed trachea. Collapsed both lungs as a result. Avulsion at the site of the gaping hole in the neck. Notice the edges of this hole, Tony. It's as if he'd been bitten by an alligator or something."

"Probably bled a hell of a lot, wouldn't you say, Doc?"

"That's another oddity. Whole body exsanguinated. Not a drop of blood left in it. Very little in the gash around the neck. If that represents a bite, it's a big one. Not a drop of blood left in him."

"From the time you got the body and the time it was found, what time you think he got this big bite?"

"Maybe one or two in the morning. That's a guess at best."

"That messes up my theory."

"How?"

"I figured the killin' was done elsewhere and the body dumped where it was found. That would say why there was so little blood on the site where we found him."

"Hard to figure. Should have been a flood around the head where the hole is."

"You won't believe this, Doc. There wasn't any blood outside the guy. And he was found face down."

"Somebody did a hell of a cleanup."

"Tell me something. Could all the blood come out of a body and clot so you wouldn't find it afterwards?"

"Normally, I would say no to that. But the things here belie that. It's like the blood was intentionally drawn off the body before the bite was made. No needle marks anywhere though. And that, my friend, isn't easy to do."

"What would they do with all that?"

[32]

"Figure seventy-five cubic centimeters per kilo, and the guy weighed about seventy kilos. Hell of a lot of blood."

"We found a couple of odd prints outside the place. Looks like they're off a big dog."

"Possible. Got to be a really big dog. I doubt if biting and chewing like that would drain every bit of blood though. Really licking the platter clean."

"I know. Sounds crazy."

"Anyhow, why a big dog? We have cats; Carolina cougars and gators around here."

"Them particular prints were made by a dog, Doc."

"Well, you have to check the dogs on the island. I suppose there are Great Danes. See if any got loose lately. You realize this dog would have had to handle locks and doorknobs."

"And what if the animals' owner was with him?"

"Sounds a bit like a Sherlock Holmes story. Or Gideon Fell. He got out of a locked room that sounded impossible to do."

"Fell? Never heard of him."

"Ellery Queen type. Authors would create impossible situations. Let me know what you come up with. I'm curious."

"Want to play detective, Doc?"

"I am curious about this one. If you find an answer let me in on it, Tony."

"So play detective but don't get in the way."

After Tony left the building, José returned to his office. He thought of how the case would excite his wife. "Wait until Pam hears about this one," he said to an empty room.

The White's lived in a modest home outside the gated communities. It was a two bedrooms, one bathroom, one powder room, one car garage, smallish kitchen and dining area located on the road to one of the islands beaches. It sat on a half acre plot with a white picket fence surrounding it. Their kitchen was small. The view from the main window was of the sound on which Breakers View Island bordered. There were seven more homes similar in architecture surrounding the house.

Pam White came home an hour after her husband. Her name had been shortened from "Pambazuko" which was Swahili for "sunrise". The Whites had met in Italy where José had trained in pathology. Her family at home in Kenya had been quite upset by her marriage to a Latino, even a professional one such as José was. She was slightly shorter than her husband, with a figure that professional models would envy. She had a turned-up nose and high cheekbones and kept her black hair cut short. Women that met her were always envious of her body, her legs in particular. The White's were hesitant about settling in South Carolina, but José's position and her school personality made any awareness amongst friends and neighbors disappear.

After relating the events of his day, he went into details about the afternoon he'd spent with Tony Pickett.

"Wow! How can you eat after that story? And you are correct. I am intrigued."

"Pam, Tony doesn't figure this one will be so easy. There's no sense to that blood loss. Some crazy Boris Karloff type scientist? Needs blood for his experiments."

"Sounds like a jagged machete to me," Pam said as she poured cocktails for the two of them.

"Could be! Like some monster took a swipe at him but missed all but his neck. I've decapitated bodies before. This was an almost!"

"Grew up where some sucker could take a machete and use it like he was handling a pencil on writing paper. Could swipe and take off an inch if that's all he wanted."

"Tell me. 'Sucker'. Is it a common word amongst the Africans? You use it a lot."

"No Swahili word for it. Nearest would be '*mbuzi*!'"

"What's that mean?"

"Goat."

"So to you sucker is goat?"

"I call 'em as I see 'em!"

"I use '*chupetes*'! Means 'dummies!'"

"Well, it's a puzzle. Don't envy Tony. No blood where there should be. Locked doors. Big dogs."

"I'd sure like to talk to Mrs. Licht. Probably piss Tony off though."

"Want to try making a baby?"

"Kid'll look like a grey Kenyan and have black curly hair."

"Be big tribal doings in Africa, you get me pregnant."

"C'mon, off with the clothes. I can hear drums spreading the news already."

She lay there shivering as his hands played over her body. He did things slowly, arousing her to a high pitch. Fondling her breasts and kissing them before moving his hand down between her legs. He entered her and they both climaxed together. After they had calmed down and while he was still inside her, she giggled.

"What a combo!"

"Was that awkward?"

"Good heavens, no! There ain't anything awkward about you when you make love, my Latin lover! I was thinking about you all afternoon. Particularly when you kissed and nipped at my neck."

Pickett and Hay entered the gate to Surfside Plantation. This plantation was the closest to the causeway to the island. As he drove, Tony thought about the new double lane highway on the island. When he'd first come to the island there had been only a two lane road that ran the length of the island. The change, with the new four lanes, made the travel time half of what it had been.

[35]

He recalled the traffic at the time the island had to be evacuated as a hurricane approached. It was the worst traffic tie-up he'd seen anywhere.

They were on the way to the Licht homestead to interview the grieving widow. Tony had called to get permission. The daughter, who had arrived the day of the tragic death, said her mother was able to talk to them. Hay carried a small tape recorder.

At the gate they obtained directions to the Licht home. It was on the ocean border with a view of the sound behind it. It was a large, pretentious house when compared to the others in the immediate vicinity. There was a three-car garage on the right side. Hay looked up at the roof and whistled.

"Big outfit! Three chimneys! Must use a hell of a lot of firewood."

"Also a lot of vehicles! Look! So many that one sits along the right side of their garage." Tony pulled up in the driveway, which circled the front of the house. The front of the structure had four pillars and was white with huge floor to ceiling windows. The landscape was sparse for the size of the house. The two detectives walked up the walk from where they had parked and rang the bell. There was an iron sculpture imbedded in the front door depicting what seemed to be a jumping dolphin. The doorbell sounded a church chime. After a wait of two minutes, the door was opened by a stocky woman whose hair was tied up in a bun behind her head. She wore no makeup.

Must be the daughter, thought Tony. She resembled the father, from what he'd seen of the man's face. Doesn't seem upset as I thought she might be. "We called to get permission to speak with Mrs. Licht."

"And you are?" The woman hesitated.

Tony took out his wallet and opened it to his badge and I.D. card. "I'm Inspector Pickett. This is my assistant, Sergeant Hay."

"Okay! She's in the library. You won't take long, will you? This is a difficult time for us."

"I'm sure it is. And you are?"

"The daughter, Sir."

"Your arrival must be a help to her. Did you get here today?"

"Captain, I believe you're asking me where I was when my father was attacked or whatever."

"Am I that obvious? I am sorry."

"I was in Chicago when I got the call from my mother. Arrived here twenty-four hours after I was summoned by her. I can show you my plane ticket."

"My assistant will check it if you don't mind. It is something we have to do to be thorough, Ma'am." Tony was embarrassed and spoke apologetically.

"My brother will be in tonight so that is enough of an alibi for him, isn't it? There was little love between my father and his children. You'll be more aware of that as you investigate I suppose. In fact, we hated him a lot." She turned, and with a gesture, indicated the two men should follow her into the house.

The foyer was somewhat bare with just a small table and mirror behind it on the wall on the right side. The library was to the left. It was quite different from the entry hall.

On three sides shelves ran from floor to ceiling, filled with books of multiple sizes. There were two easy chairs and a huge couch between them. Four lamps were interspersed amongst the seating arrangement on small tables. On the wall facing the seats was a large fireplace with andirons on the side. A small television set sat on a table to the left of the fireplace.

Anna Licht lay on the couch. She reminded Tony of the paintings he'd seen of Dutch women in their homes. Her hair was done in the same fashion as that of her daughter. The difference was that hers was all gray and tied with a black ribbon. She wore a gray dress that seemed to be too big for her

[37]

body, but it was hard to tell because she lay on her side. Her feet were covered by a small blanket.

The daughter asked if she could stay. Pickett apologized and told her they would call her for a talk after they had talked with her mother.

"Mrs. Licht, if you don't mind we are going to record our conversation. Is that alright?"

"I don't mind." The voice was surprisingly high in pitch. Tony couldn't pin down the accent. He assumed it must be German.

"I'm Chief Pickett and this is Sergeant Hay. We hate to bother you at a time such as this, but it is essential that we get all the background we can as soon as possible. You understand I'm sure."

"Chief, you sound more upset than I am."

"I beg your pardon?"

"I mean, do not grieve. We didn't get along so well lately anyhow. Even when he stayed here with me. And that ain't been so much lately."

"Did Mr. Licht have another residence?"

"Oh yes! He slept in the small room back of his restaurant sometimes. And here, in the room in back of the kitchen. I sleep upstairs in the big room by myself."

"Is there another residence is what I meant. Did he have another home on the island?"

"Where he stays when he don't come home is no matter to me and I don't even want to know."

He was uneasy about asking the next question but went ahead with it. "Was he seeing other women, Mrs. Licht? I don't mean to pry but it could be important."

"That man wasn't only seeing them. He was sleeping with them all over the island. Worse here than in Argentina."

[38]

"Could he have another family here or somewhere else? With other children?"

"I wouldn't be shocked, Officer. It's possible."

"How about enemies? Do you know of any?

"Not here."

"Oh? Where?"

"A man like Karl was always looking over his shoulder. Not only here, but everywhere he went. Probably no place in this world where somebody didn't hate Karl Licht."

"Why was that?"

"He was a '*gehilfe to the devil*.' A Nazi monster! In charge of death camps when I met him. I seen those secret papers where he tried to hide them from me. He didn't think I knew about him. But I knew! I read all the stuff he had and saw all the pictures!"

"What's in those papers?"

"Names. Places. He sent people to the chambers. He was in charge. That's what makes me and the kids hate him when we found out. I bet relatives look for him everywhere too."

The policemen were astonished by the revelation. Tony had heard nothing on the island but praise for the man. One of the biggest philanthropists. Involved in all the "Do-good" projects and supposedly quite the popular personality. He leaned toward the woman on the couch in front of him. "You are stating that he was a war criminal, Mrs. Licht?"

"Oh yes! One of the worst kind of them!"

"Think before you answer this, Mrs. Licht. Did anyone besides you and your children know about this?"

"After I learned about him, when we packed to move here, I tell Fanny and Joseph about their father. It ain't an easy thing to do, Officer. It didn't change nothing for them too much. They just hated him worse, that is all. They knew he slept with other women. Children don't like such a man. But it didn't bother me none. I don't care as long as he leave me alone."

[39]

"Did anyone else on the island know about your husband?"

"Only my kids. They know about the papers I seen."

"Did he ever mention anything about being afraid of anyone on this island?"

"Here? On this island he was *mensha*. He gives money to everything. Good old Karl Licht! Everybody's friend!"

Archie leaned over and whispered to Tony.

"Ask her yourself. I don't have to do all the talking."

"Mrs. Licht, did your husband have any Jewish friends on the island?"

"Oh yes! He made special efforts to have friends with Jews. Big money donations to their temple. Rush to give to them. I think if they knew who he was they wouldn't take his money."

"So you told nobody about his past," asked Tony.

"Office, I already told you I told nobody. Why would I want anybody to know about this family? What would they say? And the kids tell nobody. They could lose their friends." She called to her daughter. "Fanny, bring us some coffee. I'm dry from talking!"

After a short lull in the conversation, her daughter appeared with a tray with coffee and dishes. She passed cups to the officers and poured. Then she sat at her mother's feet on the couch.

"I'm sure you've heard our conversation."

"I have listened to all of it, Officer. No, my brother and I have not told anyone of my father's past. That would have been social suicide. We were ashamed. No way would we tell anyone else. But, oh, did we hate that man!"

"So nobody but the three of you, and I'm sure your spouses, knew about your father. You see what I'm getting at?"

"We were too ashamed at being related to the man. You think someone here is taking revenge? Not that I would blame them."

"Did he indicate that he was coming home that night?"

[40]

"I think he intended to come home." Anna sat up on the couch. "When he goes to another woman he takes his toilet case with him to work. It's still in that back room here."

"Those times when he came home, what time did he arrive?"

"Usually about two or so in the morning. I could tell when the toilet flushes downstairs."

"And were there times when you didn't know he'd come home?"

"Oh yes. He sleeps downstairs and I sleep upstairs."

Fanny interrupted. "My parents were married in name only for a long time before we came here. As long as I can remember."

"You really disliked Karl Licht."

"By now you must realize that."

"You live in Park Ridge, near Chicago?"

"Yes. That's where I was when mama called; with my husband, our daughter, and the maid. Dr. Hugh McGee was attending the baby who is ill. I have all of it written down for you." She handed Tony a sheet of paper.

"I don't mean to be overly pushy." He could feel her lack of patience in her voice. "We have to be thorough. Is your brother expected soon?"

"He and his wife are, or were in Vienna. They are flying home at this moment. He will save their ticket copies for you, Officer. We never told our spouses about our father. We're glad he's dead. Wait'll the papers get a load of this story. Wait and see what so called friends will be doing." Her voice was full of sarcasm.

Nice family, thought Hay. Bet the bastard sat with his back to the wall every place he went.

Tony raised another question. "Do you know if any anti-Nazi groups were onto your father?"

"I've never been approached by anyone," said Anna Licht.

[41]

"We've been through all the papers at the restaurant. Nothing there that's helpful. I have a paper that permits us to look around this house. Is that alright with you?"

With Fanny in the lead they went through the Licht home. She handed Tony a carton filled with papers. "These are the papers and pictures my mother mentioned."

"Thank you. I can assure you that nothing here will be made public unless it is acutely necessary. We'll leave it up to you and your family what to tell the public."

"The word will get out even if we don't want it to, Officer. No way to stop the papers from finding out somehow. We're ready for it and have expected it someday."

"You understand that I will have to check with the airlines and with that Dr. McGee. Routine, but necessary."

"I understand. Sorry to sound so abrupt. We've been under a strain."

"No need to apologize, Ma'am."

There were still more interviews on Pickett's schedule. Some of these were delegated to Archie Hay and other members of his staff. Tony kept the more prominent individuals to himself. This morning he headed to the Bethel Temple and Moses Pickney.

Pickney had lived on Breakers View all of his life. His ancestry dated back to Civil War days, probably earlier than that if records were obtainable. He had survived by doing odd jobs for the sixty-seven years he'd been alive. He'd remained a silent but negative critic of the way the island had changed over the years. The freed slaves who'd originally settled the island had created their own version of Utopia or Eden. But now they watched helplessly as the new settlers created a haven for retirees and tourists, with golf, tennis, restaurants, (unaffordable for them) and traffic problems with cars they could also not afford except for the trucks needed to maintain the dwelling agricultural activities that were diminishing in scope as the island was being sold by the few of them that had any of the property left.

Moe had become an island character and had been interviewed for articles in local magazines and the main newspaper on the island; all portraying him as a relic of the slave era who had a relationship to names that dated back over a hundred years and probably went further back to African ancestry as well. And for emphasis, he usually pointed out the names on gravestones in the few remaining graveyards on the island. The name Pickney was very common in the area, both on the island and on the mainland.

At the moment, Moe was employed full time by the temple as caretaker. This involved gardening, cleaning, carpentry, and occasional electric work. Tony wanted to talk with Moe, who seemed to have knowledge of any and all island activities and also many of the inhabitants. The detective parked closest to the area where Moe was working, raking.

"Why howdy there, Mister Pickett! What's the good Chief of Police doing around here?"

"You know who I am Moe?"

"Surely do! You helped my family that last time we had to evacuate the island for Agnes. That was a son-of-a-bitch hurricane, wasn't it?"

"I recall. Lucky we didn't get what they got upstate."

"Sooner or later we gonna get one a them blows right at us!"

"Wanna ask you some questions 'bout this place, Moe."

"Figured you be getting to Moe sooner or later."

"You been on this island since before the big developers come in. You know everything goes on here."

"Go way back. Before the ferry, and the bridge, and the causeway. Too bad they come along. Make it too easy to get here. Some good folks and some not-so-good ones. That also makes it easier for the not-so-good-ones to get off the island in a hurry when they have to."

A car parked next to Tony's. A tall man got out and walked over to where the two men were talking.

"Moe, this is Doctor White from our hospital. I told him he could snoop around for news so long as he stayed out of my way, and I suspect he's here for the same reason that I am. Right Doc?"

"Heard Moe is a walking encyclopedia of Breakers View and its history. Wanted some information about the place."

"Do a lot of walking, Doctor. You run the place where they take my blood testing for sugar all the time."

"Those tests keep you alive, Moe."

"How come you don't take it, Doc? Only helpers there."

"That's because I'm the head honcho. Let others do the work. Like Tony here. But don't let me interrupt. Mind if I listen in?"

"Matter of fact, I'll listen. You ask the questions."

"Okay! Moe you been reading in the paper about the man murdered in the restaurant?"

"We all reading about that."

"Ever heard about a cougar around the island? Or a mountain lion? Or even a wolf?"

"Now you know, I never seen one. But I heard we used to see Carolina cougars years ago. Wild cats died out. Deer are doomed to disappear from the building. Birds leaving too. Bob-whites gone. Houses squeezed them away. Feed them. Put up fancy bird houses for them. No more natural habitats left. We call it civilizing."

Tony interrupted what was sounding more like a nature lecture to him than a fact finding. "So all the wild life left here is birds, deer, squirrels, dogs, cats, occasional coon, snake, and possum?"

"Don't forget rats, mice, voles, skeeters, and ants."

[44]

"Definitely no wolves."

"Not I ever heard of. Course we got dogs get abandoned and form packs lookin' for food."

"Live in undeveloped areas."

"Not much of that left. Only place to be alone here is a graveyard."

"Don't quite follow you, Moe."

"You want quiet and be by yourself, be dead. Like that one gone. The man who was in the coffin we lost."

Tony thumbed through his notebook. "Coffin apparently disappeared on the way to the island. Driver picked it up at the airport and then disappeared. Found him the day we found the truck, but no coffin. He's in the psycho ward at the county hospital."

"They was gonna bury the thing here at the temple. Make it a monument to something or other. I got the spot all dug and waitin'!"

"And they lost him?"

"Plumb disappeared. Whole thing; body and coffin."

"Gone just like the cougar. No wild animals left. Used to be good turkey huntin'. Can't fire a rifle no more."

"Crazy thing here, Doc. You can buy firecrackers in this state but you can't shoot them off."

José handed a card to Moe. "You think of anything give me a call. Okay? Anything about wildlife we haven't mentioned."

"Call me first, Moe. I'll let the Doctor know." Tony was about to admonish José about getting in his way.

"What do we know about our problem, Chief?" The president of the temple had just arrived and joined the group. "Is this another deputy?"

"This is Doctor White from our hospital. Head of the germ searching department and blood sucking, according to Moe here."

[45]

"I assume he means pathology department. Can I help you with anything, Doctor?"

"We were asking Moe here about wolves on the island."

"I read about the killing at that restaurant; large dog or something. Too bad! Karl was a good friend of the temple. Generous supporter, I should know. I am the president of this congregation. I don't think we have wolves in the Sunbelt though."

"Moe was telling me about the casket you lost. Do you think it possible that something of value was in the coffin besides a body?"

"All we know is that it contained a body of a Holocaust victim. From Poland! They found a mass grave at a building site. We decided to put up a shrine to a Holocaust victim here. You wouldn't believe the red tape involved; all kinds of releases and permits. Three quarters of a year we have been working on this project. So now all we have is a pickup truck and a driver who don't know what happened to his cargo."

"So who was the corpse? Did they identify it?"

"Some poor victim, like the Unknown Soldier we have in Washington. Only this is an unknown civilian who happened to be at the right place at the wrong time in history. A bad time! Nazi time! There were apparently fifty or more corpses at a building site they uncovered. I should say skeletons. This one was quite well preserved. All gassed to death. But now we got no martyr to bury here until they find the thing."

"Is it possible that some valuable jewelry was interred with him or her?"

"Are you kidding? You think those bastards would allow anything worth anything to be buried! Particularly on a Jew! They even pulled gold teeth out of the bodies, probably before they gassed them. Those damn Poles! Worse anti-Semites in Europe; helped the Germans in all this shit!"

[46]

Pickett sat at his desk in the empty, except for him, headquarters building. His conversation with the president of the temple had impressed him, giving him things to consider that he'd never thought of before. Six million is a lot of people! He pictured a stadium such as he'd seen on television at sporting events with sixty thousand excited fans and thought about how many places would hold six million people, all Jews, waiting to be slaughtered. Men, women, and children! He pictured them all crying at once and tried to mentally compare that sound with the sound of the fans at the sporting events. Assuming that Licht was partly responsible for such atrocity, why should he try, or even give a damn about his killer? Could Licht have felt the terror that the Jews had felt? But he knew that he wanted to find the killer and would continue to pursue an answer to the enigma, even if he realized that the killing was probably justified. If it turned out to be an animal, so be it. But he had to know in any case. Such an animal would have to be controlled by a human, and if revenge was the stimulant to commit this crime then he had to expose the killer. A major question in his mind was the one about the non-appearance of blood at the scene. And he realized that no animal could have managed the entry and departure to and from the scene of the crime. That had to be controlled by a human. And the pathologist had shown him the deficit of blood in the body of Licht. No zoos in the area. No circuses. Where do I go from here?

His meditation was interrupted by the entry of José White into the station house.

"Anything new on the scene?"

"Not a thing." He motioned for José to take a seat in a chair by his desk. "All I have you know about. It's whatever Mr. LaVine told us at the temple."

[47]

"Checked the E.R. No bad dog bites or anything that might resemble one. Went back in the records for eight months and no such. Certainly can't find any news about wolves."

"I know. We checked that sort of stuff all over the area. Lots of stray dogs though according to the shelter. It's that huge paw print gets me. Got to consider a human that set this all up."

"Yeah! Someone had to have cleaned that restaurant floor up and that must have been some task."

"Want a cup of coffee?"

"That'd be nice. Black please!"

Tony poured a cup for the doctor.

"Not bad for station house fare. This has got to keep you all awake."

"Early shift makes it and leaves it for us. Usually pretty strong and shitty tasting by now. Today, it ain't too bad. Keeps me awake! And I better stay that way all that's going on these days. Usually all we got is a few drunks, fender benders, and domestic quarrels. Now we got missing caskets, corpses, drivers, nut cases, blood free bodies. What the hell!"

"What's happening with the driver?"

"Loony bin at county! Talks gibberish!"

"Anything new at the Licht house?"

Tony lowered his voice unconsciously. "Listen Doc. What I tell you is strictly between us. I can trust you not to spread this around?"

"Whoa! Don't tell me anything you don't want me to tell Pam as we don't have any secrets from each other ever. She will not spread anything, but you have to trust her and me on that score."

"I trust you both, okay? This guy Licht had quite a background."

"How So?"

"Seemed he played around with women. Here as well as in Europe and South America. Dirty pool."

[48]

"From what I've learned he was well liked here. Big philanthropist. Gave a lot of money to all kinds of causes. Even helped finance the temple."

"Well his family hated his guts. I really mean a big hate. His kids tore him apart. According to his daughter, from what she tells me anyhow, he wouldn't have made a big hit in Israel either."

"What does that mean?"

"Turns out Licht was a Nazi war criminal type. Ran a death camp in Poland in the forties. Hid it all until they got out of Europe. Made it to Argentina with a big bundle like a lot of them and winds up here somehow."

"I'll be damned!"

"If this gets out it has to be because the family spilled it. I told them we wouldn't. The wife offers nothing. She was really cowed by this guy."

"You realize this puts a new light on things?"

"I know exactly what you are thinking."

"Revenge! Someone else knows about Licht's past."

"I am way ahead of you on that, Doc! Suppose someone knew about that coffin that's missing. Had a relative in Poland that died in that way. And suppose that someone connected Licht with all this shit!"

"Wouldn't the killer want to leave a clue as to what and why?"

"That'd narrow it down too much; to some Jew. Too obvious! What would make Singleton go off his rocker?"

"Could he be the killer?"

"It's possible! He was picked up with nails and a rope, and canned goods, all shoplifted. Had a history of going around with groups that picked on Blacks and had anti-Semitic literature mixed in with other shit like that. Militia actions and crap! Crazy situation! Wouldn't have expected he'd have admired Licht!"

[49]

"There's got to be a connection!"

"All he does is blabber about cows and tape recorders. Am going back to see what else can be gotten out of him."

"Can I go too?"

"I suppose so. You are a coroner type here and involved. But listen! Don't offer any opinions. Don't want any flack about the department eliciting information through a non-official!"

"Give you my word."

"The guy's in a padded cell and under watch twenty-four seven. Can you go right now?"

"Off today. Will leave Pam a message. Assistant at the hospital is taking over today."

"I should have such a setup. Be gone a couple hours tell her."

"She'll get the message when she gets home from school on the answering machine. Want to use my car?"

"Be a hell of a lot nicer ride, but I got to keep in radio touch. Called in a deputy to sit here in station. Want to finish the coffee first?"

"Taste grows on you. Probably dissolve my teeth; had enough though."

As Tony Pickett drove across the country to the county hospital he thought about all he knew about Rudy Singleton. Despite their being heard by several professionals, no one had been able to make sense of his mutterings. Even the psychiatrist was at a loss as far as interpreting what Rudy was saying. But they kept making attempts to penetrate Rudy's thoughts, odd as they seemed.

The county hospital was an old building built so long ago that the name "Hoover" could be seen on the cornerstone. It had the look of a stone fortress with scattering areas of disrepair in the blocks that made up the walls and six levels of windows. The

[50]

There goes that nine again," said the guard. "He's been giving us that all the time."

"What the hell does nine mean, Rudy?" Tony was impatient.

"Go slow, Tony. Let me do it my way."

"You got the floor, Doc."

"Does eight hurt, Rudy?"

"Nein! Kauen meister!"

"There goes that cow and master shit again."

"Kasette!"

"See Doc! Tape recorder stuff too! Nothin' makes sense."

"There must be some meaning to what he utters, José. But what in the hell, is it? Sounds like he taped a kids show and cow was part of it." Tony had been making notes of everything that was transpiring in his notebook.

"Did you see a cow on television, Rudy?"

"Nein! Nein!"

"See, Doc! Channel nine. That's where the kids programs are, I think."

"You watch channel nine, Rudy?"

"Nein!"

"Just answer 'yes' or 'no' Rudy!"

"Kassette! Sich legen!"

"Sick leggings? This guy ain't never been known for being a great brain, José. What's all this meaning? He's had an attack of some kind, Doc."

"Let's see what we have here." José took Tony's notebook and read. "Nine, cow, mister, or maybe maestro, cassette, and now sick leggings. Boy, I bet a good novelist detective could put this stuff together."

"Well, you got him to open up a little. You are now my unofficial assistant. But nothing is done without me. Remember that!"

[53]

"We have quite a mess on our hands not that we are a team unofficially! Missing caskets and disappearing blood, and animals opening doors without keys."

They drove home in silence for a time.

"I am going to drink a great big cold martini that only Pam can make," said José, breaking the silence in the car.

"I got other things to do and think about. I got a hit and run and several break and entries to worry about. Now, I am going to give you my cell number which you will give to absolutely nobody else."

"You have my office, my cell, and my home unlisted number here in your notebook now," said José, tucking the notebook into Tony's pocket.

José retrieved his car at the station house and drove home. Tony sat down at his desk and read what he had put in his notebook. He tried to make sense at the multiple odd words he had jotted there. A desire for something alcoholic came over him at the moment. It was a feeling he had not had for a long time. The desire had caused such trouble in the past, a way of life that had left him in anguish. It had been a relief when she had left him but that feeling was only momentary. Thoughts of his failing marriage returned. It has been his fault. "We shoulda had kids!" he said aloud to nobody in particular. He then thought that maybe they'd have turned out like Licht's. In fact, he couldn't think of any relatives he had at the moment and he'd made no real close friends. Archie Hay was the closest he'd come to a confident, and now possibly José White. That would take time. For now, he would go home and finish a half bottle of scotch that had been in that state for months.

José White left Pickett at his desk in the stationhouse and drove directly to his modest home that was not located behind the gates of any plantation, but within the confines of a neighborhood of homes designed obviously by the same architect. The only differences in the houses were the front windows and doors which differed in size and shape and color. Most were limited to two bedrooms of moderate size, plus single car garages. The kitchens were adequate to contain the basic essentials and a small table with four chairs. José had often remarked that when under the influence of excessive alcoholic beverage, one would find it difficult to find one's own house. Changes had taken place in the neighborhood since they had moved in that created an air of individuality, not always successfully. The modest planting about each home had grown to overwhelming heights, and in many cases indicating neglect in care and lack of pruning. These changes were apparent in other areas of the island as well. Another change that upset José was the fact that there was a time when one did not always bother to lock up the house when leaving for periods of time to shop or visit a neighbor. He would not let Pam walk alone on the beach at night anymore. The incidence of break and entry crimes had increased alarmingly. In earlier times there had been a bridge to the island that opened to allow passage of watercraft but it was gone now, replaced by causeways giving easier egress to criminal activity. The increase in island traffic was of unsupportable proportions. None had been so naïve amongst the early inhabitants of the island as to not expect development to ensue, but none had anticipated it to happen so rapidly. The total population had increased threefold in the short time since the White's had moved to the island. It quadrupled during the high tourist season as high as ninety thousand. Build-out was close as far as housing was concerned, and now extended on to the mainland. Off-island housing was less expensive for the most part to accommodate those who worked on the island but could not afford to buy or build on the island. The result was choking

[55]

rush-hour traffic coming and going to the island daily every morning and evening daily.

José found the mail in the kitchen topped by a small Kenyan idol. A note read that she would be home late due to an after-school meeting. And since she would be driving home later than usual his supper was in the refrigerator. José was usually horrified by Pam's driving. She had to be reminded that they were not in Africa anymore and had to obey speed limits. She was still quite aggressive but he had trained her to slow down a good bit.

The *Island Sound* was on the table. It was the only local publication on the island. Pam had left late on that day and had brought in the mail. And read the paper before leaving. Jose decried the fact that the paper did not carry a depth of articles but had an abundance of reports on island sports activities. In addition, there were reports about tennis and fishing and whatever activities took place in the local elementary and high school. It angered José to read short reports about what the United States President had done or said in a few short descriptive lines followed by half a page report on a football team in Oregon or New York. The headline in today's paper was about something the town council wanted to do that was opposed by a local citizens group that appeared at the meeting of the town fathers and voiced opinions the preceding night. There were still a few farms on the island. The farmers produced roadside stand produce to sell. The farmlands had been inherited many years previously by relatives of the freed slaves of the Civil War. An article described an attack on a cow by some animal, possibly by a stray dog or a pack of the same. The owners of the cow had heard a commotion outside which had aroused their German Shepherd dog in their trailer home. It had become quite agitated, leaping at the door of the home in attempts to get outside. The next morning, one of their four cows was found mutilated in a

[56]

field behind the home. The last part of the article drew close attention by José. It seemed that whatever had attacked the cow had lapped up most of the cow's blood, leaving the rest of the carcass untouched. He dialed Tony Pickett at once and invited him to come to their home for a discussion of what he thought was a very relevant occurrence.

Pam White arrived a few minutes after he'd called Pickett. She joined him at the table since he hadn't eaten the food she'd left for him yet.

Pam was as tall as her husband with a posture that seemed military. The erect appearance gave emphasis to the shapely curves of her body. She was slim and wore her hair in a braided bun at the back of her head. When undone, the braid extended to her shoulders. She only wore it that way when not involved in school activities on weekends. She'd been a beauty contest winner in Kenya years before and still maintained an exotic appearance.

"Damn, how I hate teachers' conferences! Same crap repeated by the same individuals over and over. Now we have to make more use of computers in handling the kids. How in the hell are they going to get a bunch of sixty plus year old broads to use computers, when they can't use them except with a book of instructions along side?"

"Seems to me it should make teaching easier."

"Bullshit! Not every kid fits into a pattern. No machine is gonna tell what pattern to follow whatever behavior is going on or what psychology o use on a specific kid. You have to feed into the machine what he does in and out of school and what and how his parents handle things at home and how he gets along with siblings. And that's only part of the picture. Anyhow, what's with you?"

José stood up and embraced his wife and they kissed.

[57]

"Maybe I should go out and come in again. Sorry I sound bitchy."

"Sounds like you had a bitchy day."

"You Latinos can handle that kind of stuff. Jungle folk are not as easily calmed."

"Want a drink?"

"Scotch. I'll make you one too."

"Tony Pickett is on his way over. I called him."

"Business or pleasure?"

"Both."

"I'll drink this slowly. Goes down too fast when one is upset."

"You have it made girl. Easy job! Good supporting husband. Probably inherited beautiful looks."

"Bullshit! What's the business part of Tony's visit?"

"Remember what I told you about the missing casket and driver?"

"Yeah! Some ghoul!"

"They found the guy."

"Named Karloff?"

"Karloff was better looking than this redneck kid. And a lot saner!"

The door chime sounded at that moment. Pam answered and introduced herself to Tony and ushered him into the kitchen.

"Jeez José! You didn't mention that you were married to a beauty queen!"

"Oh, cut the crap! Let me hear why you are here. The business part! Be nice and I'll make you a drink."

"I was in the process of tying one on when you called, José."

"You must have had a day like mine!"

"You wouldn't believe the stuff your husband and I have had to deal with today."

"Hear you found the coffin thief!"

[58]

"We visited him in the county loony bin this afternoon."

"Before we tell her about that, Tony, did you read about the cow that was attacked last night?"

"Got all the details from Archie Hay! Them dogs drained all the blood outa that cow. Remind you of anything we discussed?"

"That's why I called you. Looks like we have a bunch of feral dogs. Wolves?"

Pam interrupted. "So what about the guy in the loony bin?"

"He sits all day in a trance. Gets agitated at night. I seem to be the first to get him to say anything." He handed his notebook to Pam opened to the notes of the meeting with Rudy Singleton.

"Wow! Cow? Sick leggings? Nine? Mister? Maestro? He must be a real weirdo!"

"It all must mean something to him?"

"Same gibberish! He's in some hypnotic state."

"Remember the autopsy I told you about?"

"Karl Licht," added Tony.

"Oh yeah! No blood at the scene."

"Keep this under your hat; Pam. Turns out this guy was a Nazi. In charge of death camps. Treblinka! Left Germany about fifty or more years ago. First for Argentina then here." Tony got up and poured himself another scotch. "I interviewed Licht's widow. She hated him and so did her kids."

"Reminds me of that play we saw, *The Little Foxes*."

"Then I discovered the corpse in that missing coffin is, or was a Holocaust victim. The island temple was gonna create a shrine. I think there's a tie-in with the murder of Licht. Some relative of the victim seeking revenge on the Nazi!"

"Nutty way to take revenge. What did he want with all the blood?" asked Pam.

"Also locked doors. A sleuthing puzzle," added Jose.

"Got an idea. Be right back," said Pam. She left the two men in the kitchen.

[59]

"Another drink, Tony?"

"This is the first time in a long time, José!"

"Had a bad habit once?"

"Really bad. Long time ago."

Pam returned to the kitchen and placed two large books on the table. "Hand me those gibberish notes again, Tony."

"Got the problem solved?"

"Not yet. Got an idea based on what you tell me about that family though."

"So what's what?"asked José.

"Patience buster! You suckers had it right in front of you. You missed the boat. You all may get to like me after I am through with you!"

"Go on," urged her husband.

She turned the pages of the large book on top and copied things down on a sheet of paper she held.

"Look here, suckers!"

"I'll be damned. She's got it, Doc!"

"She sure has. I'm amazed honey!"

"See, it's German. Cow and master are really *kauen meister*. *Kasette* is coffin. *Sich legen* is lie down. *Nein* is nine but not the number but negative. You idiots are too phonetic!"

"Masticate master. Casket! No! Lie down! What the hell!"

"Chew master! Eat!"

"And when he says negative, he was answering my questions," exclaimed Tony. "So he's saying his master should lie down in a coffin."

"Pambazuko, you are a female genius and I am happy to lie down with you every night."

Over many Southern wetlands low tide brings with it an odor usually described as "rotten eggs." At night, the aroma is accompanied by a cacophony of insect sounds that peak in intensity at midnight. All creepers, crawlers, and fliers emerge, emitting sounds that can be heard over vast distances of wetland. Reptiles leave their daytime cover to seek food. Birds and bats arrive to get food from the supply of insects that have exposed themselves. Nature supplies a convention of sorts, with a choral group to announce its presence.

At the side of the wreck Delilah, there was another sound caused by the rhythmic lapping of the water against the derelicts hull, which was coated by slime and mud. There was a strong smell of sulfur in the vicinity of the wreck. The full moon was the only source of light on the scene, interrupted intermittently by passing clouds. There was no wind, which added to the intensity of the odoriferous concentration in the area. Few nocturnal animals invaded this area of the swamp. Mosquitoes would have exsanguinated them if the stench didn't repel them.

Inside the hull of the wreck all was still. The base was filled with a foot of muddy, foul smelling water, and mosquitoes. Rudy Singleton had placed the crates in a row to support the casket that he had been accused of stealing and it was kept above the water level. To the side of this was another long box that had been Rudy's resting place before his capture by the police.

At half past ten a vapor cloud began to flow out the sides of the casket that rested on the crate platform. The lid of the coffin slowly elevated, opening as if being pushed from the inside. As the opening increased, so did the vapor density. It coalesced into a definitive cloud about two yards in diameter. This cloud flowed out of the rotting hull into the night air. The appearance of the cloud on the outside of the Delilah seemed to cause a hush in the noises of the swamp. It was as if Mother Nature had appointed an orchestral conductor to silence the sounds of the swamp by laying down the conducting baton. The cloud drifted off toward the edge of the area and disappeared suddenly as an object seemed to fly out of the mist and drift towards Breakers

[61]

View Island. As it disappeared, the orchestral sounds of the insect population resumed as suddenly as it had halted. Rats appeared, invading the hulk, as if appointed as guardians.

Joab Jones, as a teenager, had lived in Louisiana in the Lower Delta area below New Orleans. He had little formal education and had spent several years in reform school as the result of many quasi-criminal activities. On his release, his mother and several children had moved to the Low-Country of South Carolina. She worked as a domestic on Breakers View Island, and her four children were employed as laborers, maids, and waitresses. Joab, her eldest, was a refuse pick-up man, a job he detested. He claimed that only Blacks were available for it since nobody else would do it. One day, he read in the local paper that a bus company was being formed and wanted experienced drivers to take local people to shopping areas, the mainland airport, and various destinations. Joab Jones was hired.

The island had needed transportation other than private automobiles. There were taxi services, but many retirees couldn't afford them and were too old to drive themselves. Some of the private retirement complexes did provide busing, but there were many retirees who did not live in those units that needed transportation. There was also a large off-island population of employees that needed transportation to the island other than private cars which had created an immense traffic problem with rush hours in the mornings and in the evenings which, after the Chamber of Commerce complained to the employers, was addressed by the bus company's formation. Designated bus stops were set up for residents outside the gated communities and in shopping areas throughout the island. Regular schedules were set up, but even with these, it was difficult for residents inside the gated communities to get to the stops. But most agreed that what they had was better than nothing.

Joab Jones was assigned the West View Plantation area. This included the two shopping malls and trips to the small airport at the north end of the island. In the Northeast, particularly in the New York City area, there had developed a rift between Blacks and Jews. This had some effects on the island. Acts of vandalism occurred at the temple. These were caused by imported rabble-rousers. Local Jews said, "What else is new? It has been going on for several thousand years." Once Israel declared itself a nation, things changed. There were still pockets of anti-Semitism and the Arab world would probably never accept Israel. There were anti-Black groups as well, particularly in the South. The Ku Klux Klan still existed. But, for the most part, the few non-achievers were outweighed by the achievers. Joab Jones was part of the non-achiever group that hated Jews.

Jones found that belonging to such a hate group exhilarating. It gave him a feeling of importance. What really mattered to him was the sense of excitement at the meetings with cronies who felt the same. He helped paint swastikas on tombstones, fences, signs, and broke windows on temples on occasion. These acts were performed off-island since there were no strict Jewish cemeteries on Breakers View Island. It was a constant "Halloween Night" of vandalism for these hate groups. The local Jewish group did not want publicity given to these deeds. It was better not to publicize the acts and let the furor die down.

Joab had another shortcoming. Imbibing alcohol left him somewhat unmanageable. He would denounce Jews to anyone within range of his voice. It was after his employer cautioned him and threatened him with the loss of job that he changed his attitude some but not altogether. He would not lower the step platform to the bus when given folk with obvious Jewish names to transport and often passed them at pick-up sites, claiming he'd not seen them waiting. His name was brought up at the temple for discussion at times. He was a blatant anti-Semite. Something should be done, but nobody wanted to make a public issue of the matter and it was dropped.

There were only two passengers on Joab's van-bus by nine o'clock that night. A couple was returning from a local restaurant and had hired the van to take them back to their home instead of a taxi.

"Y'all eat good?"

The man answered. "You bet! We ate at the Claw. Not only good but reasonable."

"What'd y'all have?"

""The works in one big dish. Lobster, shrimp, clams, plus a good wine!" answered Murray LaVine."

"That'd keep me in the john all night!"

"You know your limitations, Joab. Bet you eat a lot of things that wouldn't sit well with me!"

"Just meat and potatoes!"

"He eats anything as long as it's edible. I never saw such an appetite!" offered Flo LaVine. She was short and chubby.

"I can't afford things like that. Like you people can. You got the money. My people don't!"

"Nonsense! There were several Blacks eating there."

"Uncle Toms! Make money for the White people."

"That's not true anymore."

"You found that coffin you lost, Mr. LaVine?"

"Nope! Only the truck and the driver, who turned out to be a little nutty!"

"Rudy always a little crazy!"

"Why would anyone want a casket with a poor dead Jew inside?"

Joab kept quiet. He thought to himself that there was no such thing as a poor Jew. This bastard eatin' and livin' it up while we

[64]

"For what?"

"For not getting me up too!"

"Well, you check the bars where he might have stopped at this end."

"And what do I do about the B&E I'm working on, and them two fender benders? Need to interview the driver of the Buick. Sounds like he was really quite drunk."

"Make this a new priority. Send Green to cover the other shit."

"Boy! Paper's gonna love this one. Missing bus. Missing truck. Missing coffin."

"Got an A.P.B. out. You'll have company looking for the damn thing. Try and keep things as quiet as you can."

"Suppose I got to check that damn swamp again. Them damn bugs!"

Tony stayed at his desk after Archie left to type up the latest report. He often projected himself into a fantasy world at this desk. If he could only pull a quick one here! Media will be at him soon enough. Need to get a reputation! Need to get the fuck out of this resort and into a big city department. This crap! Missing kids, coffins, vehicles, wife beaters, and mostly drunks on vacation. Typewriter! Why the hell can't they get me a computer? I'm probably too stupid to use one. Could get White's wife to teach me. Damn rich island kids drinkin' to all hours. Traffic. And now this! Missing buses!

"Lay down and chew the master!" He said aloud to himself. "Get in the coffin at nine!" Made no sense. Rudy was really off his rocker. We should get a dream psycho dream interpreter. And wouldn't the media have a ball if they learned we asked for help. And with the airport being over the state line we could get the Feds in on this. That's all we need!

The phone rang. Billy had found the missing bus.

"I'm on my way!"

[67]

Pickett drove to the rear gate of West view Plantation and spoke to the guard on duty there.

"It's a little dirt road, more like a wide path. Just beyond Judge Ervine Way. You've probably driven by it a million times and never seen it. Dark as hell at night there. About two miles down the road, Tony."

Judge Ervin Way was named after the Civil War era plantation owner. On the island, in some areas, there were still ruins of slave quarters deep in the wooded areas. This particular area of the island was inhabited mostly by a Black population. Many had inherited the land from ancestors in the previous century. Tony drove slowly looking for the road sign. He finally spotted it in a cluster of weeds and wild flowers. The sign read "Salamander Drive" in barely discernable letters. Tony thought the mail delivery to this spot must have a hell of a time. The road was barely wide enough for his patrol car. He followed it for about a hundred yards to a small clearing on the left side of the road where he spotted two patrol cars parked. Deputy Rice opened his door for him.

"How'd you find this damn thing, Billy?"

Billy Rice was an older member of the force. He'd been a ferry hand before the bridge was built. He was obese and had a large walrus-type mustache.

"Used to be a wooden statue of a saint or somethin' right near that sign told you the name of the street. Couldn't hardly ever see the damn thing, but I always made it a point of lookin' at it when I passed this way. This mornin' it's gone so I stop to look. Someone ran into the statue and it's layin' over there. Saw tire marks and got out to check. Ain't touched nothin'!"

Archie Hay was standing on the other side of the van which was parked deep in the growth.

"Wait'll you see what we got here, Chief!"

[68]

"Need a machete to get close. Billy, call in and tell them where we are."

Tony walked through the waist-high growth and opened the door. He and Archie looked inside.

"Holy shit!"

"Gee Tony. I only seen that sort of thing in pictures."

"Billy, call the lab boys and the E.M. folks. No question but what he's dead, but someone got to make it official."

The two men walked away from the van, leaving the door opened.

"Whole shebang on the way. Photographers too!" Billy had returned from using the radio.

Tony was angry. "What the fuck is going on on this island? I'll bet nobody ever seen what we just seen in that vehicle. Gotta develop a stomach for this shit! Let me know when they get here, Billy."

Tony and Archie entered the vehicle. The four rows of seats behind the driver's seat had been laid back, creating a vast cargo space about fifteen feet in length. On top of the folded down seats was a long board about ten feet long. On top of the board was another board at right angles, shorter in length and creating a large cross. On top of this structure was Joab Jones with his arms stretched out. Nails could be seen holding his hands to the cross boards.

"Son of a bitch! Crucified!"

Jones throat was torn away from the neck. His eyes were opened and the face had been stamped with a look of horror. This was the scene that confronted the lab crew. Checks were made for finger prints and many photographs taken of the scene, including the area around the van.

"Can we pull out the nails and remove him now, Tony?"

[69]

"Yeah! Be sure to save those nails. Take all that shit with you. Don't see the log he was supposed to have. Tell the examiner I want a rush job on this one."

"We can probably trace the boards. Look new. From some construction site!"

Tony and Archie walked back through the woods behind the scene as far as the border to West View Plantation where there was a barbed wire fence separating the community from the rest of the island.

"Can see why nobody builds here. Damn bugs!"

"Someone has to know the layout back here pretty well, Arch. Has to have known about this spot. This is Black country. Think we may be dealing with the brothers here. Some major feud!"

The battery of the van was dead and the vehicle had to be towed out of the growth area. They found nothing else in the area but empty beer cans and many used condoms.

"Whoever screwed here had his ass bitten but good."

Tony laughed at the remark. "Should look for a hammer and more nails. The damn log book ought to be laying around here someplace."

"Great place for kids to make out."

"Kids make out different than I used to these days. Look at them rubbers. All over the place."

"We got us another wolf, Tony!"

"No way, Arch. Wolves don't use hammers and nails. We got a real psycho!"

"How about some animal comin' by after the fact?"

"And closes the door after him?"

"I know what else you gonna point out."

"You noticed that too. Some on the boards. Not much though. Bet that body's empty. Like that Nazi bastard!"

"Bet that's why Joab's naked."

[70]

"How about somebody and his animal? And why two guys who didn't know each other get killed by having their throats tore away?"

"Both involved in drugs maybe?"

"You get the leg work. Bars! Check out the Wilson girl. I want to talk to LaVine some more. He's overly on the scene, Arch. Loses a coffin and now is the last one to see Joab alive. Check that Baden Baden guest list. See who had dinner last night."

"Don't think we've missed anything."

"Private eyes in books never do."

"That's why them guys have editors. Case they miss something."

"Watch yourself, Arch. This killer don't fool around. Some of these bars don't like honky cops asking questions. Don't want to start civil rights shit arguments. Damn it all. Got to type up all these damn reports."

"Tell me what some of these words mean, Doc." Pickett was in White's office. He'd brought the coroner's report for José to see.

"In essence, it means the wound was similar to the one on Licht. Made by some large animal. Nothing here says what happened to the blood."

"Some nut is setting up a blood bank in a way that leaves something to be desired."

"I've thought of something, only you'll think I'm a nut case."

"No way, José. I need all the help I can get."

"Thought about it all night. It's crazy but I can't think of anything else."

"Let me decide what's crazy."

"Nothing else could really explain all this."

"So?"

[71]

"I was thinking of an abnormality in the animal world."

"What?"

"A giant bat. A real blood sucker!"

"And how does this bat open and unlock doors and move trucks?"

"Got a better idea?"

"We got us a mad killer human. A throat cutting, blood sucking, son-of-a-bitch!"

"And how about cattle? He like to suck that kind of blood?"

"Gotta admit it's hard to tie all this shit together. But no animal hammered them nails!"

"I admit that this killer does some non-animal things."

"They gave Rudy that truth drug. Same crappy gibberish. That seems to be all they can get out of him."

"How about the missing coffin?"

"All we got are those German words. Now Rudy never learned no foreign language in his life. Barely talks good English!"

"So he's no help!"

"Well, we got zillions of other worries! Shoplifters, auto accidents, petty larceny cases. Pot showing up everywhere. Got seven deputies working their asses off."

"Sounds like you have to expand a bit."

"Don't I know it. This don't sit well with the town council. Bad for tourism!"

Pickett returned to his office. Hay was waiting on him.

"Got the stuff on Jones?"

"Jones was born in Louisiana in some little town below New Orleans. Got out of reform school as a teenager. Should have had three to five but got malicious mischief and family. Mom and three kids moved here. Spent a year away from family in Baton Rouge. Back again and worked for a refuse company. Didn't like garbage and got hired by the bus company. Common-law wife is Annie Wilson. Lived in a trailer on Fallow Street. No kids!"

"What's the wife do?"

"School kitchen. Serves lunches."

"Spoke with her yet?"

"On my way this afternoon."

"Fallow's not far from where we found the van."

"Same area."

"Meet you here later. I'm gonna talk with the LaVines."

Fallow Street was in the Black section of the island. Very few White families lived in this area. Despite pressure on the town fathers, many roads were unpaved and homes had septic tanks rather than sewage connections. Most were converted motor homes sitting on cinder block bases, usually surrounded by rusting wrecks of automobiles. Some had fenced in yards and made some attempt at landscaping. Annie Wilson did not live in one of these later types.

Archie drove slowly along the unpaved road, which was made worse by rocks and ruts and stretches of muddy puddles. An unsuccessful attempt had been made to plant some type of shrubbery around the home. The original yellow color had faded to a milky dirt hue. Hay thought how awful it must be around the outside after a heavy rainfall. There were no trees near the trailer. He parked and went up to the door of the motor home and knocked several times. No response.

"C'mon Miz Wilson. I know you're in there. Have to talk to you."

"Miz Wilson, if I have to break in to see you, it's gonna be police trouble for you. And who's gonna fix the broken door then? Sure not Joab!"

The door opened slowly to the length of the bold chain.

"Mister Jones ain't here. He's dead!"

"I know, Miz Wilson. Let me in. Just want to talk with you a little." Annie's voice reminded Hay of the maid in *Gone With The Wind*. High pitched and sort of screechy sounding.

The door shut while the bolt was being removed and then opened slowly to admit the officer. Archie climbed in over the high front step. There was a small sitting area at the entrance. To the left of this was a small kitchenette. He could see a bedroom at the far end beyond the small kitchen area. A small lamp stood at the right of the sitting area by the door. He had noticed the electrical lines outside leading to the motor home. Most electrical lines on the island were buried, but not in this housing area. He had also noticed a small outhouse behind the unit as he'd driven up.

"Nice place you got here, Miz Wilson."

"Nice enough. Don' wanna stay here alone no more with Joab gone. Noise outside every night. Drunk niggers all over the place. Seems like nobody here sleeps anymore!"

Annie was about five feet tall and stout but not obese. She had black hair tied back in a bun and was wearing a green dress covered by an apron, which appeared to Hay to be a picture of a lake on it. She wore slippers at the moment and no stockings. Her only jewelry was a pair of earrings shaped like frogs.

"What you gonna do with Joab gone now, Miz Wilson?" She had taken off the apron and he could see that she was quite pregnant.

"We never thought about getting married. I should have somethin' comin'. Been with him a year or more now."

"There's a legal term for it. You shouldn't have too much trouble." Hay noticed a flag with a swastika hanging on the wall in the back of the sitting area. He pointed to it. "Was that Joab's?"

"Yeah! He collected all kinds of queer stuff." She was no longer apprehensive.

"Did he talk about the Nazis? Did he like the Germans?"

"Oh yeah! Mostly hated Jewish folks. Sounded off about them all the time. Pick on the brothers up North. Ran around with a bunch felt like him. Gave him books to read 'bout Jews. He got a letter from the folks what come from that temple. Tell him to please calm down. Amazin'! He shut up for awhile! 'Cept when he was drinkin'!"

"No kids?"

"Not yet. Bastard left me with one on the way though. Poor Joab! He ain't never gonna know what bein' a poppa like! What I gonna do? His mama want me outa here!"

"Where's his mama located at?"

"She a nurse at the hospital. Got a license to be a nurse helper or somethin' like that. Lives in one of them places hospital built for workers. Real cheap!"

"You get along with her?"

"Pretty good. She want Joab should marry me only he don' want no part of that. He not happy about me bein' pregnant! I cry a lot. But not for Joab! For me!"

"You got no family around here?"

"Nope! Got some friends. Had folk over for pizza couple times."

"Know folks that really didn't like Joab?"

"Give you a list a mile long!"

"Know who wants him dead?"

"He fight all the time. Over in that bar! The Calibogue Bar across the bridge. Every week has a fight there."

"I know where it is."

"Usually beat the hell out of somebody there. Learned that chink way of fightin'! Learned from some club he belonged to. Club gonna save America!"

"Beating them up! Make somebody pretty mad at him?"

[75]

"He egg somebody into a fight and really beat the poor bastard up."

"He keep any papers or records around here?"

"Not I know of! Nothin' but flags, boots, knives, and clubs with German crosses on them."

"Did he ever mention the name Licht?"

"Nope!"

"Well you be careful here alone, Annie! And thank you for answering my questions."

"Expected the police! Crazy way he got his self killed! Joab was a great man in bed though. 'Cept look what he left me with!" She patted her abdomen.

"Don't show much yet!"

"Probably be a boy like his daddy!"

"Your first?"

"Had one Chicago long time ago."

"Get rid of it the hard way?"

"No. My mama made me give him up for adoption."

"Hope Joab's mama gonna help you, Annie. Have that grandson so she can remember her Jaob!"

"I hear you talkin' officer. This kid gonna be all what's left of Jaob."

Archie Hay sat at his desk doing the report of his interview with Wilson. Paperwork was the most disliked task the men had. His notebook contained all the info about the multitude of cases he'd been assigned and he referred to it constantly as he worked, sipping the awful black coffee available from the office.

"Let's see what we got here," he said to himself aloud. His thoughts went to the absence of blood on the murder victims. Two dead guys and no blood! Can't see any dog or anything lapping up that much. And how does a dog move that van around back into the woods? And what is suckin' the blood outa them

will be jumpin' in a few hours when rush hour starts, he thought to himself. He perched himself at one of the bar stools.

"Drinkin' on the job?" asked the bartender as he walked slowly to the site where Archie sat.

"Nope! Just want to ask a few questions."

The bartender was a huge obese man. He must have weighed in at least two fifty or more. The two customers at the other end of the bar turned away from where Archie sat and sipped from their bottles of beer and conversed in muffled tones.

"Guess you heard about Joab Jones?"

"Must have missed it in the paper. He from around here?"

"I got sworn testimony from folks who say he was a regular customer in here."

"May have been."

"So don't give me any shit!"

"Look, I just didn't recognize the name!"

"You want to talk here or shall we go down to headquarters? Hate to have to close you down!"

The big man shrugged his shoulders and said nothing.

"In fact, it might keep you shut down for a week or more."

"Actually, it seems I have heard the name mentioned couple of times. Yeah! I recall now!"

"Stop the bullshit! I know he had regular fights in here and lots of 'em."

"That may be so, Officer!"

"I want to know who with!"

"Seems I recollect a few disagreements. In fact, I don't recall the names though!"

"When was he in here last?"

"Maybe four or five nights ago."

"Who'd he fight with?"

"Seems like a fella names Moe. Yeah! Moe shouldn't sass Joab! Joab rantin' bout folks he don't like and one punch and Moe's down!"

"What was the fight about?"

"Probably nothin'!"

"Musta been some reason!"

"Joab just liked to fight! Ain't that right, George?" he addressed the two men at the other end of the bar. They ignored him as if they hadn't heard him.

"We're talkin' to you, bud. Suggest you answer."

The nearest man turned toward Archie and put both hands on the bar as if to show he had no weapons.

"I hear you. Jus' don't recognize the name!"

His companion rose and walked in a shuffling manner towards Archie. He was about six and a half feet tall and almost as huge as the bartender. Archie put his hand on the handle of his revolver in an obvious motion.

"I'm Emil Lewis. I know Joab. He is a mean bastard and really no good. I didn't like him and I don't know anyone who does. Why Annie stays with him nobody can figure. Never heard he hit her, but I bet he does. And I sure don't want to get mixed up in this shit and I am leaving." He and his companion walked out of the bar, leaving some money on the bar for their beers.

"He one of those guys Joab fought with?"

"Hell no! Joab don't fight with nobody he can't beat. And nobody beats Emil!"

"So the only one you know who fought with Jones was Moe?"

"I recon so!"

"You sure have a bad memory. I ought to take you in!"

"Jusus man! I tryin' my best! I am getting old and my memory don' work like it used to. Probably have a disease!"

"Yeah! Call it wise guy fever or somethin'."

[80]

"No! I am really tryin'!"

"Well, try harder. I close you down your boss ain't gonna be happy."

"Seems Moe don't like to hear dirty talk 'bout his boss."

"And who is Moe's boss?"

"He caretaker for that Jew church on the island. Near the bridge. Moe sayin' how they was gonna bury a dead one in back of the place from overseas and Joab say why don't they get a Jew from here and if they couldn't find one he'd get one for 'em."

"And Moe didn't like that?"

"He says so and that got him a whomp in the belly."

"Here's what I am gonna' do. I am putting my name on the top of this sheet of paper with today's date and the time of now. Be back tomorrow. In the meantime, your gonna have the whole list of everybody had a fight with Joab waiting for me, and where they live. And a whole list of everybody hates Joab or got beat up by him. You got that? And if that list don't make me happy or ain't ready, I am gonna close you down which is gonna upset the owner of this place and you will be in the tank for a real cop session of questioning by meaner cops than me. Joab is dead and you don't have to worry about getting beat up by him."

"Do the best I can, Officer! You gonna get me in deep shit when folks around here hear what I have told you and what you want on this paper. But I can handle that! How that bastard get his self killed? Don't read the papers much."

"You should! It's all in there. What's your full name?"

"Amos Foster! I live in the back of this place in a motor home. Alone!"

"Bet you ain't always alone."

"I entertain occasionally," he yelled at Archie Hay as he left.

From the time he'd sent Archie to the Calibogue Bar, Tony Pickett had been with the LaVines. The couple lived at the north end of the island on West View Plantation. He'd called ahead to arrange a convenient time for an interview. He'd been told to come as soon as possible and he had.

The house was a match for about eight in a row, obviously designed by the same architect. Small two bedroom affairs with one-car garages on the left side of each. The streets curved in an almost circular fashion which probably made it difficult for strangers to find their destination when visiting the area. Each had a centrally placed chimney and almost matching landscaping in the front. The mailboxes were all located in the same spot relative to the house and all of the same color and shape. Covenant rules usually dictated the type and color of the mailboxes in all the gated communities on the island. Tony pulled the patrol car he was driving off the street and parked in front of the house. Covenant rules called for all four wheels of parked cars to be off the street. It made sense when one considered how narrow most of the streets were behind the gates of the plantations. The ruling also kept most residents from planting lawns up to the street edges.

Florence LaVine was napping when Tony arrived, so he and Murray met and spoke in lowered tones in the front living room. The room had two sofas and two easy chairs. A television set sat across from one of the arm chairs with a long coffee table in front of it. The other half of the room was a dinette, small, and separated from the living room by a large shelved divider. There were unmatched cups and saucers on the shelves. There was wall to wall carpeting of rust coloring and two small floor lamps on either side of the easy chairs.

"You must have had a lot of red tape to deal with in Poland."

"You wouldn't believe what we went through. It was worse actually with the U.S. authorities. Such diplomatic maneuvering!

Treblinka wouldn't cooperate at all so we went over their heads right to Warsaw. That too, took a lot of talk, letters, cables, long distance calls. Such red tape!"

They were discussing the difficulties of getting a body released to the temple for the shrine on Breakers View Island. To avoid having to take notes, Tony, with LaVines approval, had set up a small recorder on the coffee table.

"Then we had the U.S. to contend with. The health departments we had to clear with you wouldn't believe. There must have been six or seven of those. I never filled out so many forms in my life. Things are easier dealing with the Polacks now with Russia gone. I think somebody figured the good publicity of cooperation would be better than the bad publicity of saying no."

"Where the hell is Treblinka anyhow? Not in my atlas."

"It's not on most maps. On the river called 'Bug' which probably was an appropriate name. Not too far from Warsaw. Most of the Jews sent there were exterminated. Towards the end of the war when photographs were taken of the place; they were really ghastly."

"If it hadn't happened, I wouldn't have believed you could have gotten this far with a dead body from Europe. It's an amazing story."

"I agree! We figured it would be an impossible task and would need help from God to get things done. Timing was the thing. Since way back, Poland has been very anti-Semitic; one of the worst in Europe. But money talks and they needed our money. Amazing, isn't it? Trainloads of Jews coming in and none coming out and the locals didn't know what was going on. I can tell you, Officer Pickett, there is nothing I hate worse than an uncircumcised European Polack. This was good publicity for them. Doing something good for Jews."

"How did you and the others react when the expose of Karl Licht came out?"

[83]

"I'll be honest with you, it wasn't that shocking. I had correspondence about him a year ago. Weisel found out who, what, and where about him. The whole congregation was informed."

"Did you know the man?"

"Not intimately."

"And now what is your reaction to the killing of another known anti-Semite, Joab Jones?"

"Again, Jones was not news to me. I mean about him being a Jew hater. B'nai Brith, that's our watchdog organization, knew he belonged to such social groups. I think there are still members of such outfits around. I spoke to him and I thought I might be getting to him."

"Did you like the man?"

"I pitied him. A typical one of 'life's losers.'"

"Did you or anyone you know talk about putting a stop to his behavior?"

"Put yourself in my shoes, Mr. Pickett!"

"But do you know of any person who might have been forceful about it?"

"What are you getting at? Should I incriminate myself or anyone else?"

"So why is the question so surprising? Here are two known anti-Semites who met violent deaths recently."

"So!"

"So consider my position. What would you be asking?"

"It is possible a Jew was involved. Revenge! I see your point!"

"It is certainly a possibility."

"So how can we cooperate with you? You want a list of the temple members? You going to investigate them all?"

"If it becomes necessary."

"Let me tell you something. There are a lot of Jews on this island who are not members of our congregation."

"You make it look like the old needle in the haystack inquiry. What would you do in my place?"

"First I would talk with our rabbi. Ask him to give a sermon on the evils of revenge and explain why he is giving such a talk."

"You think the perp would want the world to know why he committed such crimes?"

"Don't assume so much. Why does it have to be a vengeful Jew?"

"Consider the state of Israel. Enemies on all sides in the Middle East. Terrorists would love to get the public to think like you are."

"Now you're muddying the waters!"

Flo LaVine entered the room at this moment wearing a robe over a night gown. "I heard you talking."

"We're discussing our missing victim."

"Officer, do you think there is a connection between our missing corpse and these crimes on the island?"

"Yes I do, Mrs. LaVine."

"I heard you talking about Joab Jones. Murray tried to lecture him on the bus. Joab did some sadistic Halloween pranks. Stupid acts of juveniles!"

"There is nothing intelligent about following mob stupidity. They felt they were wronged somehow. I was assigned many civil rights activities before I settled here."

"The world is still full of such stupid people. In spite of all the facts about Hitler and the Nazis that have been proven and exposed. There are still many who adopt such philosophy. You know there are developments where Murray and I couldn't buy a house still. And how many country clubs do not admit Jews, Blacks, or even Italians?"

[85]

So a lot of things were not solved in the Civil War, were they, Mrs. LaVine?"

"So it is still a lunatic world we live in. It'll take two or three more generations to wash it all away, particularly in the Middle East. If ever! But I tell you frankly, Officer, if I am in a car and Karl Licht is walking down the street and nobody is around to see, I would run him over. And even back up over him to make sure. And the same for Joab. So am I a suspect? Multiply what I have said by the hundreds of Jews here and off this island."

"That's crazy talk, Flo! You want to get us involved?"

"Bullshit to you, Mister LaVine! Licht ran a place where I personally lost several relatives. God knows who else did!"

"Forget her talk, Mister Pickett! She has been with me every night for the past two months and couldn't be involved."

"I agree with you on that score! Tell me, have either of you recalled seeing anyone else on the bus the other night?"

"Absolutely not! He missed our stop and had to back up to it. He even said we were his last customers. Nobody else was aboard!"

"Did Joab seem apprehensive?"

"Not in any way."

"He didn't mention that he had to stop anywhere else?"

"Nope!"

"And after you got off, he didn't make any unusual turns that you saw?"

"Nope."

"Okay! I do want that list of congregation members though."

"You want to pick it up here or should I bring it by the station?"

"I would appreciate if you would drop it off at headquarters."

"Maybe we should put an asterisk by the names that have numbers tattooed on their arms!" said Flo, sarcastically.

[86]

The man entered the office just as they were getting ready to close down for the day. Cozy Nest Rentals opened only one evening a week until nine thirty. It was off-season now and there was very little activity as far as rentals went, so they had decided to close shop even earlier than usual. The office consisted of two rooms in a tiny building, set back from the main island highway. There was an unpaved driveway leading from the road in a semicircle. There was very little in the way of landscaping around the structure; a few bushes that needed watering and one pine tree to the far side of the building. One employee sat in the front room at a small desk. On the other side of the desk there were three small folding chairs. There was also a small table in the room with magazines spread haphazardly over the surface. In the room to the rear there was another desk and files, and a small bathroom. A small table held an electric coffee maker. Two women were working the evening shift.

The man entered without knocking or ringing the bell outside. The secretary at the front desk looked up from where she was filing the day's activities and saw a tall, thin person wearing baggy jeans which were obviously too big for his body. His hair was quite long and almost hid his entire face from view. It was straggly and uncombed as if he'd been out in a strong wind before entering. She thought this odd, as it had been an extremely calm, hot day outside. The man's face was covered by white stubble which seemed to obscure all but the eyes.

Ida had worked for the realtor company for several months. She was single, having lost her husband in the Vietnam War. Her short brunette hair was arranged in a pageboy, and she wore no make-up. Ida was obese and not particularly attractive but apparently did not care to put any effort into making herself look better with make-up.

[87]

"I assume you are still open for business?" The voice was a deep guttural, rasping pitch. It sounded to Ida like a prolonged gargle.

"Yes," she replied and motioned to one of the chairs opposite her desk and he sat down on it. The accent was definitely foreign, but she was unable to identify it.

"Want long term rental of unfurnished place. Quiet and not near road. One bedroom; very quiet place please."

She pushed a sheet of paper from her desk towards him and handed a pen to the gloved hand. "Please fill out this form, Mister - ?"

"Opfer. Hans Opfer!" He looked at the sheet she'd put in front of him and studied it for a few minutes. He then slowly wrote in each section of the form quite deliberately and slid the sheet across the desk back to her.

"You gonna use a credit card?" The hand writing was almost illegible.

"Not familiar with what you ask."

"It's to pay for the rental. We require a months' security."

"I pay cash; paper money. Here!" He held a huge bundle of rolled bills up in front of her. "Take what you need."

"We show the place first. What time can you be here in the morning?"

"*Nein*! In the morning! Only tonight! You show me tonight. Pay extra for special trip by you. Take a day's rent out of total cost, for you, now. Must settle tonight once and for all." He turned so that his face was now opposite hers. She looked back at him and seemed transfixed by the eyes that stared at her. There was a moment of silence.

"May! I am going to show this gentleman a rental now. Cover for me. Mister Opfer wants to settle for cash now. The papers are on my desk and completed, and the money is here too." She called this out to the woman in the rear room. "I am taking the keys and the contract. I am going to show him and will go home from there. You lock up!"

"Okay! Will do!" answered her co-worker. Mae thought it was odd that Ida would show so late but a buck was a buck and for cash she'd probably have gone too. Must have been a good size tip. Besides it was off-season and they needed the business. She did sound strange though!

"We can go in my car." Ida led the way to a small coupe. "I'll bring you back to your car when we return. I will show you how to get there."

"I have no car!"

"Is your taxi gonna wait?"

"No taxi. Let us go please!"

Ida was now frightened. This guy could be a rapist or something. Suddenly she felt compelled to do as he asked. "Did you have a specific location in mind?"

"Just quiet place out of the light."

"How will you get your luggage there without a car?"

"I will worry about that. I will quite manage everything."

She drove slowly. "I think we have just what it sounds like you're looking for. It's a very quiet location in a very quiet plantation. There are four villas in a row on one side of the street but houses across the way. The villas are small. The salesmen use them on occasion for overnight prospects. Customers! There is some worn furniture."

"Condition of furnishings do not bother me."

Ida drove into a small grouping of tiny villas located in a semi-circle across from three large homes, only one of which was occupied at the moment. The villas were on the side of the street that bordered the ocean, which was about two hundred yards back. Plot lines were laid out all the way back to the ocean. Very few trees were in this developing area.

[89]

She parked and they got out of the car and she unlocked the door to the villa. There was a small kitchenette, a sitting room, one bathroom, and one bedroom. The bedroom would be too small for a king size bed.

"Not too much closet space. There is another closet near the front door for your overflow. Dishes and stuff are in the kitchen. Want to check the place?"

"*Nein*. This will do very well."

"No garage. It's a carport. That one big pine will protect your car somewhat though. I can show you other places. You're paying me overtime so it's no problem."

"We see no more. This will do, *Fraulein*! Give me paper and I sign. Give me keys. Our business is finished."

Ida put her briefcase on the table in the sitting area and took out several sheets of paper. She gave him a sheet and asked that he sign the contract. He handed her a roll of bills and told her to take out what was needed for ten months and security and whatever else there was to pay for.

"Take for your troubles what is a months' rent also; for yourself."

This made her think him a realtor inspector sent to trap her and she hesitated to take any money for herself. "You don't have to do that. We get a commission."

His eyes caught hers and the two stared intently at each other for several moments. She reached out and took the money from him and placed it in her purse. Without speaking further, she handed him the keys and the map she had brought with her.

"This will show you around; where things are for shopping and so forth. Here's your copy of the contract. I encircled where you are on the map so you can find your way back when you tour the island."

"You are good worker for your employer."

"If you want to rent a car I can get you a discount."

"Have no need for a car, or your map. This location is embedded in my mind now."

"How are you gonna get food? It's a long haul to the stores from here."

"I will manage."

Ida drove to her apartment very slowly. She sat in her car after arriving and thought of the evening's adventure. How did he get to her office without a car? No means of transportation. She had lost the groggy feeling she'd had when in Opfer's company.

In her apartment she studied the contract he'd signed. He was from New York. No phone number. Didn't want a phone in the villa either. Shaking his hand was like picking up a cold washcloth. Says he expects to move on to duties elsewhere after the contract term ends. Skinny bastard! Probably some type of junkie! How was he gonna function without a car? And no luggage! Just a paper bag! Not my problem! To hell with it.

That same night, Rudy Singleton somehow escaped from his cell in the county building. A pickup truck was also stolen from behind one of the island supermarkets. It was red and similar to the one Rudy had driven to the island from the airport, which was now parked behind headquarters on the island.

At three in the morning, two figures made their way through the marsh that led to the Delilah. They pulled several of the hull's planks away from the wreck and dragged a long box out of the vessel. It was loaded onto the back of the red pickup truck.

Thirty minutes later, the guard at the gate of the Surfside Plantation stopped a red pickup truck. A face from inside the truck caught the guard's eyes and he stiffened momentarily. He then waved the truck into the plantation. It drove to Opfer's newly rented villa and the two figures dragged the box inside the villa. The box was settled into the bed. The truck departed, driven now by only one occupant.

[91]

For the second time in ten days, five shops were robbed. Only cash was taken even though a fully stocked jewelry store was one of the victims. There was no sign of break and entry. No windows were broken. No doors had been forced. Tony was baffled. Employees were all exonerated. A men's store was also robbed the same night and only men's clothing had been stolen.

Ida drove to the villa the next day after the rental experience as she did with all rentals to check on the customer satisfaction. No one answered her knock. The shades were drawn. She supposed he had hiked on a long trip to a store for supplies and left a note to let him know she'd been there to check on things.

It was quite still around the site of the villa at nine that evening. The sky was quite overcast with dark clouds which obscured the moon. A slight breeze came from the ocean. There were no streetlights on this or any of the other plantations, adding to the darkness of the night. Inside the villa, all was still in the bedroom where the large box rested on top of the bed. A wisp of smoke appeared at the edge where the lid met the body of the box and rose upward on the left side. It swirled like a miniature tornado and then condensed into a thick, dark cloud. As if controlled by a switch emitting a wind, it disappeared and Hans Opfer stood in its place.

He glanced around the room. "Much better atmosphere here for sleeping."

He turned toward the front door of the villa and disappeared, and in his place was a vapor which drifted through the crack of the door. A few seconds later a large animal, wolf like in appearance, ran across the adjoining golf course at a loping gate. It kept to the shadows and headed toward the few farms that still existed on the island.

The note that Ida had left in the doorway was on the ground, torn to shreds.

[92]

"Another fuckin' cow last night!"

"I tell you, Arch, someone is getting a lot of cholesterol these days."

"Nope! Sirloins maybe though!"

Pickett had arrived at the station house only minutes before his deputy. Both had been up since dawn and busy all day.

"Some bitch opened Watson's, the men's store. Nothing busted getting in. Opens a window from the inside and jumps out with a load of men's clothing. Opened window set off the alarm, but the bastard had run off."

"So how'd he get in?"

"For sure, not the way he got out!"

"Inside job? Employee?"

"So why jump out a window to leave? He got a key and all."

"Beats me!"

"Me too! Mayor is after me. Press thinks us nuts. Tourism is being affected. Chamber is pissed off. High season is coming and everybody wants something done!"

"So what we gonna do now?"

"They gonna call in outside help. Make us look like fuckers!"

"Makes it harder for me to get your job."

"This shit keeps up there may not be one for you to get."

"So what we gonna do next?"

"Check the employees. Most live on the mainland. All got alibis."

"Makes things difficult."

"By the way. Our friend Rudy got out last night."

"Thanks for tellin' me."

"Crazy event. Walks up to the guard at dawn and wants to be let back into his cell. Guard had a shit hemorrhage. Didn't know he was gone!"

"You got to be kidding!"

"Hell, no! Guard was floored! Have no idea where he went or why he bothered to come back."

"Maybe the son-of-a-bitch ain't so nutty after all."

"Got out without a key. Nothing busted!"

"Must have had help!"

"If so, how'd they manage? Guards heard nothing, saw nothing. And they ain't new on the job, Arch! All veterans. Nobody suspects our team guys."

"So if everybody is on duty, how did he get out? Place is all locks and bars."

"Never less, he's out. A store gets robbed! Nobody knows how the robber got in."

"Coincidence?"

"And what's Rudy do? Fly from county lock-up to the island and back? We're talkin' thirty or so miles!"

"So where did Rudy go while on his vacation?"

"Good question!"

"We really gonna suck ass if they call in outside help!"

"I know! I know! Seen Moe Pickney again yet?"

"Headed that way now."

"Call in from that temple."

Hay parked in the rear parking area of the temple and walked around to where Moe was working in the front carrying trash to be picked up by the truck that collected for the county.

"Heard I should be expectin' you, Mister Hay."

"You broke any laws yet?"

"None I gonna tell you about. Ask away. Tell you anything I know you don't! Don't know anythin' about what happened to Joab except what's in the paper."

"So you spoke with the bartender at Claibougue?"

"Told me he told you about Joab and me having a disagreement. Done nothing about it though. Ain't near Joab since that disagreement!"

"So you had a fight with him?"

"Got the shit beat out of me too!"

"Where'd you go after the fight?"

"Bed!"

"Alone?"

"Nope! Caliloo there too."

"Never left the house?"

"Never after I go to bed. Sleep's what I do best."

"Bet Caliloo don't think so!"

"You win that bet. She never complain yet. For an old man!"

"What was the fight about?"

"I guess you mean the one I had with Joab. That night it was Nazis. He usually find a way to fight with somebody. How good they is for the world and how bad Jews are. These folks have been mighty good to me, Mister Hay. And to my family. I been this color all my life and he says they call me 'black nigger' and really hate me. Wanted people in the bar to help bust up the temple. I ain't gonna stand for that kind of talk. I say shut your mouth and he belt me in the belly. Did a good bit of pukin' afterward."

"He was nice to Annie Wilson I hear!"

"That was the only thing he was ever nice about. Never beat her."

"Did a lot of bad mouthin' though?"

"Always talkin' niggers, kikes, Jew-bastards. Also ginzos, wops! Names for everybody. Better off without him around."

"But nobody has the right to kill, Moe!"

"I didn't kill him."

"And he didn't get himself killed so nicely."

"Like it says, a man sows like he reaps!"

"So what have you heard about the missing coffin?"

Arch walked over to the hole and pile of dirt. "This is where you were going to build the shrine?"

"Yep! Got a monument all made up to set over the spot too. It's inside that shed back there."

"So who do you think done him in, Moe?"

"Don't have any idea."

"How about your employers? They mad enough to do him in?"

"I don't think they even thought about Joab."

"He drove a bus and they rode in it."

"Kept his mouth shut those times. Would a lost his job."

"Couldn't one of these folks have heard about him elsewhere and be angry enough?"

"That's far-fetched, Mister Hay."

"Suppose one of the brothers he fought with got on that bus."

"That'd mean-!"

"That he'd open the door for a brother."

"Nobody wanted to tangle with Joab."

"But with a gun?"

"What about that nailin'? You think Joab gonna sit still for that?"

"I'm gonna have to talk with Caliloo."

"Expect you will!"

"Need her to say you were in bed with her."

"Hell, nobody else be in bed with Caliloo. She may haul off and slug you one for askin'. Then you stick her in the pokey!"

Archie Hay hated the leg work involved with his occupation. If only the bastards in charge would get them a computer. Save a lot of time. Damn glad I ain't in charge of things right now. It's Tony's neck on the line, not mine. There are times I really wouldn't want his job after all. This shit has sure got me baffled. And so is everyone else, it seems!

Doctor José White sent an email to an old friend in Poland. David Brodsky was a United Nations representative stationed in

Warsaw. His assignment was to follow up on the settlement of displaced refugees from any source following wars, riots, epidemics, and other upheaval causes. He sent monthly reports on these matters to the U.N. headquarters in New York. Brodsky and White had been roommates in college. White had asked him to be best man at the wedding when he and Pam Pambazuko were married. They had kept in touch ever since, but hadn't seen each other since the wedding.

In his email communiqué, José had asked Brodsky to try and get information about a recent uncovering of a mass grave near Treblinka. He included all the details about the request that had been made for a victim's body to be buried in the United States as a memorial to holocaust victims. Could Dave see if he could get information about whether any of these bodies had been identified? Time was of essence.

The following is a transcript of the reply that was received by Jose White within a week of the request.

Dear Pam and live-in companion,

How nice to hear from you both! So José, you are a full time head of a department now! Remember, I knew you when! Big shot now! I remember when all you wanted was to be an M.D. And now you run something that sounds important. I suppose you will soon be the superintendent of that school where you teach, Pam. What an aggressive team! Moving up the ladder regularly I suppose. When you get tired of him, remember that I am available, I run a sort of department too! And I have no marriage prospects as of yet. Life is pretty good here. The standards of living keep improving. They still have a long way to go though. Locals are not too friendly. I guess it's my last name! There's still anti-Semitism here but way down deep. Jokes about dumb Polacks no longer hold true either anymore. They aren't warm and gracious but they sure aren't dumb anymore. I have pretty much overcome the language difficulties by now and am getting along pretty well. In fact, the unshaven legs of the broads are beginning to look good to me. The climate you can have. Seems like it's always winter. And that's damn cold at times! Great summer resorts! And now I'm up for a transfer. Learn the language pretty well and being transferred to Guatemala, so it's back to Spanish. Now to your question, but let's not forget to update me about you.

The grave you refer to was accidently uncovered by a builder starting a housing project. It was during the excavation process for one of those endless barracks-like things. They're pretty prevalent in this area. It's the main type of architecture; all homes look alike in every detail and rowed up endlessly within a few feet of each other. It provides cheap housing and that is necessary here. It's not hard to find destitute families everywhere and that's what these developments serve. Finding them is what I do for a living in case you forgot. So anyhow, a human skull was uncovered which put a halt to the digging by machines. It was done carefully after that with shovels and hand labor. More and more skeletal remains were uncovered until the entire gravesite was opened. Took about two weeks. About two hundred corpses were uncovered. Thing was about sixty or seventy years old. Government tried to hush the news up because these folks are very sensitive about that sort of stuff. But it got out and went all over the world. Israeli reporters swarmed over the area. London News reported it in detail. I'm surprised you didn't hear about it. Revelations about the holocaust are not welcome in these parts. Locals claim they didn't know what was going on. Anyhow, the digging kept up with Israeli reps. watching closely. No I.D.'s were made. One of the bodies was fairly well preserved even with the arm tattoo visible but the records of these numbers are not easily interpreted. There's just none available for most of these things. But I will check on the

[98]

and into the trailer where the vapor condensed into a thick fog that drifted back to where the girl lay asleep and snoring in the same rhythmical pulsation. The tall figure of a man seemed to evolve out of the smoke and leaned over the inert figure of Annie Wilson.

"Annie! Annie Wilson!" A raspy whisper came from the figure which caused Annie to stir slightly and eventually roll over on her side from the flat position she'd been sleeping in.

The voice became louder. "Wake up, Annie Wilson!" It sounded as if a frog had learned to speak with a human voice. It was as if the speaker was clearing phlegm from his throat. The name was called out again, this time a bit louder and that caused her to open her eyes and stare at the eyes above her head. They seemed to glow from within and she was unable to move her stare from them. She made no outcry and being suddenly awakened just lay there staring at the two strangely lit orbs above her.

"You carry his child, Annie."

"Yeah, that's what he left me." Her response sounded somewhat like a Gregorian chant, on one tonal level without variation.

"You know it cannot be, Annie Wilson!"

"I know!"

"It would be an evil thing like its father. It must be done away with, Annie Wilson!"

"Yes! It would be an evil thing!"

"You must accept this, Annie!"

She hesitated slightly. "I do! I do!"

The figure disappeared and the vapor took its place, only much thicker, drifting over the figure of the girl who removed the slip she wore and laid back on the bed.

"It's time for us, Annie Wilson!"

[103]

"I know! I know!" She lay back on the cot and pulled her legs apart and the cloud covered her entire body. "Oh that's nice! That's better than any I got before. Oh yes! Don' stop, never!"

She breathed heavily and had beads of sweat on her upper lip now. The smoke covering her grew thicker. "Jesus! Don' never stop. Please!"

The smoke seemed to draw back off the girl's body and her legs came together as she lay there in a trance like condition with a vacant stare on her face. In the place of the vapor now appeared a large animal, which advanced toward the inert figure on the cot.

Tony Pickett was on the radio with Archie Hay. "We goofed! We never looked into the glove compartment of Joab's car. Got to be thorough! Better check it out, Arch!"

"Will do. There's car wrecks like that on most of those lots in that area. His car runs though. Adds to the ambience of the area. How you like me using them big words?"

"Still bucking for my job, Arch?"

"Got to sound like I had a higher education."

"Get your high sounding ass over there before she goes to work in that car."

"She got it runnin'?"

"Mac says she brought it over and he got it going. She got whatever Joab left behind which ain't a hell of a lot."

"Well, I think she is a nice girl, I like her. That bastard was just that! A bastard."

Hay drove out to the back road behind Breakers View Island's north end. It ran from the rear gate of Surfside Plantation down to the main road that ran down the center of the island. He drove onto the lot that housed the trailer that Annie Wilson occupied. It was elevated off the ground about three feet, based on a prop of cinder blocks as a foundation. The car was still parked where it had been on the left side of the motor home. That meant that Annie had not gone to work yet.

She's gonna have to work till that baby comes, thought Archie. Then what is she gonna live on? Gonna need help, that's for sure.

The car was ten or eleven years old and looked like it had been driven in one of those contests where they bang into each other until all but one are out of commission. The door was locked.

He walked over to the front door of the motor home and knocked. Then he banged heartily to rouse Annie. "C'mon Miz Wilson. Don't play with me again. I know you're in there. Remember me? Sergeant Hay! Spoke with you about Joab. Don't make me break down the door. Who's gonna fix it now Joab gone? I need the key to the car! Gotta check the glove compartment. Open up, Miz Wilson!"

Hay then walked to the rear of the unit and standing on a basket he found there, peered into the rear window. He almost fell off the basket and ran to the patrol car, to the radio.

"Christ Tony! We got another body here at the Wilson's! Bring the pass key thing with you. Get the E.M. and the lab boys too! It's a crime scene thing. God, what a mess!"

All arrived within fifteen minutes of Archie's summons.

"Them windows never been washed but you can see enough. Been bangin' on the door. Looked in the window in the back. What a mess!"

Tony walked around to the rear with Archie. After seeing what had so startled Archie Hay, he walked back to the front and told the deputy standing there to break down the door to the motor home. That person took a pair of handcuffs from his pocket and smashed the door window, reached inside and unlocked the door after sliding back the added bolt lock.

Archie and Tony entered the unit. Hay opened a closet in front.

"Empty."

They made their way to the rear.

"Oh my god! What a shit!" exclaimed Tony.

Annie Wilson lay naked on the cot. Her eyes were opened, staring at the ceiling, seeing nothing, obviously. Where her lower abdomen had been was a huge, red-rimmed hole, with intestines spilling out. Hay ran out and vomited outside in some bushes. Tony ordered the rest of the crime crew to get to work.

"Locked from inside!"

"I'm aware of that, Arch!"

"Really made me sick! Sorry about that! I liked her!"

"Don't need a coroner or José to tell me a large animal did this one! That hole was made by a wild animal all right. A really big one!"

"Not much blood either, Tony!"

"Sopped it up real good! This one's gonna bring outside help now. Son-of-a bitch! For sure!"

"Been here a good long time, Doc. Never seen so many bodies!" Pickett was watching José White performing an autopsy on the body of Annie Wilson. The room was located in the basement of the hospital on the island and was dark at the moment except for the area around the table on which the Wilson corpse lay. A bright light hung from the ceiling above the body illuminating the limited area the pathologist stood bent over with gloved hands and white coveralls. He'd been asked to perform again this autopsy as the county coroner was away again. White was speaking in a monotone into a microphone connected to a tape recorder on a small table behind him. After about fifteen minutes of dictation, José stepped back from the table.

[106]

"Never planned on a lot of forensic medicine. Should really write this up for publication. Amazing! All this on a small, barrier island!"

"Glad you're getting the experience, Doc. I can do without it though. Who needs this kind of shit on a resort island? Know what's gonna happen now? They're probably gonna bring in outside help. New investigators! There goes salary raises! The council is really down on us!"

"So what different from what you are doing is outside help going to come up with?"

"Oh, I'll get put in charge of coordinating everything, but some other bastard will get the credit when this is busted open!"

"I know exactly what you mean."

"Works that way in medicine too?"

"Doctors are more subtle. One guy does all the work and research effort and the running around. And then about four other department members add their names to the article and the original investigator gets his name at the end!"

The two walked out of the autopsy morgue and went to the elevator. "Let's go to my office and talk," said José.

"Glad to get out of there. Hate the formaldehyde smell. Jars with pieces of people! Ice boxes holding more people waiting to be cut up."

Tony lit a cigarette as they sat at the desk in José's office. He had tried to give up the habit, without success, many times.

"It was an interesting autopsy. You didn't realize it, but I was astounded at first!"

"Why was that?"

"Something was missing!"

"From what?"

"The girl's abdomen."

"All I saw was a belly with a hole in the middle."

[107]

"I had removed the chest organs and the intestinal tissues. There should have been something there that wasn't."

"Shit! Don't play games with me! I don't know what is supposed to be where in there. Looked like others I seen to me!"

"Nope! There wasn't any uterus!"

"You mean something didn't eat what was on top and had to dig down to get something he liked?"

"Exactly! The womb was gone."

"And the baby that was supposed to be in it was gone with the womb."

"I would say she was a couple months along; probably more than that!"

"So we have an animal that pushes aside other tissues to get at the uterus."

"Seems like that was all he wanted."

"Hell of a way to do an abortion."

"Yeah! There are easier ways to terminate a pregnancy!"

"She wasn't completely drained of blood like the others. However, I would have expected more blood in the abdomen than there was."

"Probably full by then; didn't want to overeat."

"Discovered one other thing, Tony. On her neck! May have been strangled first!"

"By an animal?"

"And there were puncture wounds on the neck. On the left side! They weren't made by any animal because the same teeth did not get used for what was chewed up in the abdomen."

"So what's that mean?"

"There had to be two animals."

"Another one drank up the blood?"

"Not all of it. Some!"

"So now we got us a serial killer what drinks blood and performs abortions the hard way."

[108]

José got up and went to a closet in his office and then returned to his desk chair. He sat silently for a while and then apparently made up his mind to say something he'd been reluctant to say to the police officer.

"Tony, Pam and I have been talking and studying something. I want to tell you what our subject was."

"When the lady comes up with an idea I listen now!"

"Yeah! She did figure out that Rudy was talking German!"

"He's been listed as terminal and is dying."

"Heard he got out for a while!"

"Superman! Bent the bars like they was candy and managed to squeeze his body between them."

"Insane people can often do superhuman things."

"I suppose! So what did the lovely lady come up with?"

"A vampire!"

"A what?"

"Vampires! Like in the movies!"

"You both gone crazy?"

"Sounds a bit like that."

"Sure does! You both gone a bit nuts on me."

"Think about the pattern of events that have taken place, Tony."

"I am! And if I told anyone we were talking this way, we would wind up in a cell like Rudy."

"But I can explain a lot of things that are happening in this way."

"Calling your idea far-fetched would be an understatement, Doc! It's downright stupid an idea! We can't play games in the crime business like the funny papers and the movies do. I tell my staff we got fairies and brownies to deal with, what do you think they'll do? I get my ass kicked from here to Baltimore!"

"Calm down, Tony! All I ask is that you hear me out."

"I'll listen. But I gotta warn you! I don't go for nonsensical shit! Not in my line of work. We got to prove everything we do and have to show facts to judging authorities."

"You're dealing with locked doors in these cases?"

"Yeah! Locks, padlocks, and no keys!"

"So how did someone or something manage that?"

"If I had the answer, I would be on the way to finding out a lot more of what's involved in this shit."

"Okay! Now listen! And damn it, don't interrupt me!"

"It will be difficult, but I will listen."

"In fictional stuff about vampires, they can change to a gas or vapor and pass through cracks or keyholes at any time."

"You really lost your marbles."

"And they can fly like bats!"

"So what?"

"So that's how they get around so fast and easy. And it could be a 'he' or a 'she!'"

"Man! You and the little woman have gone ape on me!"

"And here is the significant thing. It can change into a wolf!"

"Oh God damn! So how does one get rid of this thing?"

"Got to find it first."

"And then what? Garlic, crosses, mirrors? I seen the movies too."

"I haven't a clue at that point."

"I know what I'd do. Pull out my Colt Cobra and empty it into the 'he' or 'she'! You use a cross and I'll use a gun and we'll see which works best, Doc. I never heard such nonsense comin' from a professional what went to school after school to get where he is. Bet Pam mentioned Voodoo also! Something from Africa! I am surprised at both of you!"

"You know, Tony, I think you're upset because some of it makes a little sense."

[110]

"You can make everything fit somewhere if you try hard enough."

"The cattle. Blood gone but not eating the meat. Killer craves blood to exist. There is a creature in nature that preys on domestic animals and guess what its name is. Vampire bat! Scary thing with huge incisors. Makes a hole and then laps up the blood. An adult vampire bat can lap up five tablespoons a day. These things are usually found in Latin America, but I suppose a bunch could fly upward from there with the globe getting heated up the way we are told it is. Colonies of these things can number in the hundreds. Feed on cows, pigs, horses. Not much bigger than a sparrow too. Follows rivers and waterlines to get around from one place to another."

"This bit you're quoting from some encyclopedia makes more sense than that other shit!"

"And they operate at night when their prey is asleep. They do have enemies! Owls! Oh, and listen to this! We found it in our research. They've been known to feed on sleeping humans."

"So now we got a bat epidemic. What else?"

"There's a danger of spreading rabies."

"Granted all this stuff is facts, Doc. I'm sure you and the little lady read up on it all. You know we can invent crazy things to explain crazy things, like religion, for instance! No other way out of a jam; turn to God. It's God's will done this. And where do we start looking for random missing coffins?"

"We thought of that too."

"No more nutty stuff!"

"No! This all started after that coffin disappeared."

"Not right away but after a while."

"Then we think that's the coffin we're after."

"Man, you two are really into this. I suppose while we are noseying around we better carry crosses."

"I would say something like that!"

[111]

Tony crushed his cigarette out on the edge of the wastepaper basket by José's desk. "Gonna stop this habit one of these days. I spread this shit around I get drummed out of the service. I think what we got is an insane lock picker who may think he's one of your creatures. Personally, I think the blood is being dumped someplace. Sooner or later this bastard's gonna make a mistake and Poppa Tony gonna grab him. And I won't have to soak him in holy water. Whatever you do, keep this shit between the three of us and we'll start working on something. On what, I haven't the foggiest idea. God damn, I sure hate the smell of garlic!"

Ira Silman was the spiritual leader of the congregation Bethe-el on Breakers View Island. Although he had been raised in an orthodox atmosphere, he now espoused reformed Judaism that matched the temperament of the island's Jewish community, most of whom had migrated to the island from the Northeastern United States without any affiliation and now found that they wanted to belong to this newly organized religious organization to offer a balance to the many Christian churches on the island. The rabbi's sedentary vocation had not affected his physical condition due to his indulgence in weight lifting, jogging, and exercising in a regular program that he had designed for himself. Neighbors were able to set their clocks at seven thirty every morning as the rabbi jogged by their residences. He was tall, muscular, and well coordinated and actually gave lessons in karate to a large number of students. He was a speaker at many municipal affairs and a member of the local Rotary Club.

Hedva Silman was almost as tall as her handsome husband. She was a brunette with Grecian features coming from an ancestry that originated in Athens. Her vocation was journalism and she wrote a social column for the island newspaper and had had two children's books published. The Silmans had no children, nor did they desire any. She performed the duties of a religious leader's wife; visiting ill parishioners, attending meetings, organizing female groups connected to the temples affairs, and accompanied her husband whenever necessary in his temple and civic duties.

One of these was dinner at the home of the president of the congregation that night. Florence LaVine was disappointed to learn that Hedva had another commitment that night and that Ira would come alone. Flo had prepared a sumptuous meal, using her best dishes and silverware, which was a rare thing to do on her part, as she only used good china for special guests. Despite the fact that the rabbi was the head of a reformed congregation, Flo had come from an orthodox background and served a kosher meal. No butter was served with the bread and the pot roast, and no cream with the coffee.

"That was some meal, Florence! I'll have to go some extra miles tomorrow morning to work it off!" exclaimed the rabbi, pushing back his chair from the table slightly.

"How about an after dinner brandy, Ira?" asked Murray. He led the way to the room the LaVines called a study. There were two overstuffed chairs and a small desk with a chair that fit under the desk. One wall was a completely shelved library from floor to ceiling filled with tomes, mostly unread, but placed for show to fill the site. Handing the rabbi a snifter, Murray poured brandy, and then one for himself. Florence remained in the kitchen, cleaning up.

"Plenty more when we run dry."

"I think we should stop making a public fuss about the casket, Murray. People are not happy over the constant attention and it doesn't show us in good light. It's bad P.R. Let's create the monument to all victims of the holocaust and dedicate it in that way and let it go at that."

[113]

"I think you're right. It isn't like a piece of uninsured mail got lost. Even if it had been insured, I don't think we should have made a claim."

"Isn't that interesting about the Licht family? Sort of a coincidence!"

"Listen! Flo's family had some victims to that monster. The whole island is waiting that we should make a statement of some kind. From the president of the temple or the rabbi. Something like 'Good! It couldn't have happened to a nicer person.' I think we should lay low and say nothing. The letters to the editor are doing it for us. You read them? They're on our side all of a sudden. Why take chances on reversing the flow of sympathy? I recall when Israel was established when I was a kid. Jews who celebrated were censored by the goyem for showing allegiance to a country other than this one. It's okay to take Kathleen home to Ireland where her heart has ever been and to send money home from here to help other economies, but let one Jew sing praises for Israel and it's if you don't like it here leave! But it's been like that for a thousand or more years. Nothing is going to change it."

"Life under the Nazis must have been horrible!"

"Listen! The king of a Scandinavian country put a yellow star on his sleeve to show sympathy. Those poor folks were not alone altogether."

"Couldn't have been easy though. Doing things like that when surrounded by a bunch of sadists."

"So Ira! You ain't much of a martyr type!"

"Dead I am in no position to help anyone."

"I agree. I would not make a good martyr."

"Six million were martyrs."

"But not willing ones!"

"I am amazed that history doesn't show that more were willing to change their religions."

[114]

"We Jews have had a chip on our shoulder forever. We dare the world to knock it off. Only now with the way Israel reacts the world knows we are not going to sit still anymore and allow the chip to get knocked off. That's what the existence of that country does for us all."

"Tell me why you went reformed."

"You have to live in the present, Murray. Every Jewish celebration is a rehash of history. Same words and acts year after year. That's why we lose kids. Boredom! We keep up with the world in all other ways. Why not religion?"

"Did your parents agree with you?"

"They've modernized a good bit. Listen! I still maintain old fetishes. Here, let me show you." Ira stripped to the waist. Under his shirt he wore a shawl type cloth. It hung down front and back with an opening for his head in the center.

"This is called 'arba kanoth'. It's fringed, considered holy. All orthodox males wore one in Europe. Not much anymore. It's my personal fetish."

"Never saw one before."

"Doubt you ever will. I wore one as a kid and at the seminary. It's an old world custom. Good luck charm. Just a lifelong habit I've had and I would feel undressed without it."

The doorbell interrupted their conversation.

"Excuse me for a minute, Ira."

Murray walked out of the room and down the hall to the front door. As he opened the door he switched on the porch lights. They did not go on. "I'm sorry about the lights. Didn't know they were out." He addressed whoever the caller was. The figure was back in the shadows.

"No problem. I am fine," was the reply. The voice was extremely hoarse. It was a raspy sound. The figure on the porch stood back so that Murray could not see anything but the shadow with brightly lit eyes that seemed to be anatomical headlights.

"Is there something I can do for you?"

"A contribution. I want to make a contribution. You are president and to you I want to give it."

Murray was unable to place the accent. It was familiar in a strange way. Not a Southern drawl certainly. "Won't you come in please? I am sorry about the light."

The man entered and stood back from the room light in the corner. He wore dark trousers and some sort of dark jacket. He extended his hand toward Murray. In it was a large packet of bills wrapped in a paper binder. "For your monument to the dead. You do a good thing. World should not forget. Me, list as unknown donor. No name. Use this for whatever you want in temple. It is a good thing you do!"

Murray took the packet from the figure, startled at first. The offering hand was like touching a piece of ice. The man was quite anemic! Murray looked at what he held in his hand.

"These are all one hundred dollar bills, Sir! Come into my study and I will give you a receipt for tax purposes. I need to know your name for that."

"I am Hans Opfer. No receipt. I pay no taxes!"

"If only that were true for all of us. Please come in, Sir! There's someone here you should meet." He walked toward the study. "Ira! Come here. There's someone you should meet." He walked towards the study. "A huge donation has just been made to our temple."

"Let me put my shirt on."

"Don't bother! That shawl thing will impress our donor."

Ira Silman walked into the foyer.

"Say hello to Mister Opfer! It's a coincidence that you're here to accept this generous offer."

As Ira walked into the foyer's lit area, the strange figure let out a howl and staggered back into the dark area of the foyer, covering his face with his arm.

[116]

"Wait, Mister Opfer!" yelled Murray. He ran to where the figure had stood. Finding no one there he opened the front door. "Where the hell did he go?"

"Nobody outside," called the rabbi.

"Not a soul in sight!" answered Murray.

Florence had run from the kitchen. "What was that screeching? Sounded like you stepped on a cat's tail!"

"It wasn't a cat, Flo! It was a man! At least, I think it was a man. So where is he? Come inside, Murray!" the rabbi called out.

"I am definitely coming back in, Ira. What did you do to scare him so?"

"Those shiny eyes never looked at me. Only my scarf! Something frightened him!"

"Here's what happened to the porch lights. They've been unscrewed. He didn't want us to see him."

"I am worried about this money, Murray."

"You think it's stolen?"

"Let's go into the study and look at what we have here."

"It's a lot of money in a bank wrapping."

"What money?" asked Florence, coming into the study.

"The man that was just here made a big cash donation to the temple." Murray laid the bundle on the table, removed the wrapper, and started counting the money. "My God! There's twenty-five, one hundred dollar bills here. I hope it ain't stolen money!"

"See what's printed in the wrapper," said the rabbi. "Liberty bank! And below that it says 'Porclain House!'"

"That's what was in the paper. One of the stores robbed yesterday." Florence picked up the paper and pointed to the article.

"We better call the police. Wonder why he left the name on the bundle."

"Maybe he can't read," said the rabbi.

"Oh, come on," said Murray.

"I mean English. You heard his accent!"

"And he must have a hell of a cold. Sounded like a frog in his throat."

"So call the cops, Flo."

"Wonder how he spelled that name?"

"He wanted the donation to be anonymous."

"Funny, he took one look at my shawl and screamed."

"So what were you two doing? Comparing muscles?"

"Ira was showing a shawl thing he wears under his shirt."

"It's called an '*arba kanforth*', Florence."

"My papa called it a '*tsitsis*'. It was a lucky piece for him."

"It's also called a '*talith katan*'. Four fringes. Worn as a talisman. Sure scared our donor."

"This we give to the police." Florence took the bundle of money and placed a rubber band about it and put the whole thing in a plastic bag.

"Our prints are all over it."

"The ones that aren't ours will belong to the robber or donor or whatever!" added the rabbi.

"If it turns out it ain't stolen and it goes to the temple, don't mention the guys' name. He wants it to be anonymous."

"Can't figure out why my garment should frighten him so. Nothing more than my underwear!"

Florence walked back into the room. "Deputy is on his way."

The police car arrived ten minutes later. The deputy took the bundle and gave Murray a receipt. He made notes on the description given by the group of the evening's event.

"Chief Pickett will want to talk to you folks tomorrow. If it's convenient can you be at headquarters in the morning?"

[118]

The rabbi looked out the front window. "We'll be there. You'll want our prints, I'm sure. Did security say anything about a car racing through just now?"

"The back gate is closed as they are fixing the timer. But I was at the front gate talking to the guard. No cars came in, fast or slow, or went out same."

"This guy must have come on foot. No car in front of the house."

"He moved pretty rapidly too," added the rabbi. "If he can move that fast, he makes a pretty snappy robber!"

"I realize how inconvenient this is, sir," said Tony, addressing the president of the temple. Tony had amassed a group for that purpose. The discovery of the stolen money had necessitated the fingerprinting of the attendees at the dinner at the president's home. Florence LaVine had been the first to be fingerprinted because she had a pressing appointment elsewhere and left the headquarters building.

"No problem, sir. I can understand how essential this must be, under the circumstances. I only hope we didn't smudge out whatever prints there were on the packing." Murray LaVine was wiping his hands on the towel provided by the deputy taking the prints.

"We won't know about that for a few hours. I feel badly about depriving the temple of all this money. But it definitely was stolen stuff. Amazing though! Nothing broken into and no prints at the scene. No alarms were set off either. And it's the same at four other robbery sites in the mall. That money hasn't shown up yet either. Whatever rewards are offered, you will get. Please understand that!"

"Thank you, Mister Pickett! I will accept any reward as the president of our congregation. It will be applied toward a shrine to Holocaust victims we are erecting at the temple."

[119]

"And he ran off without saying a word?"

"Not only ran! He absolutely vanished into thin air! He must have been on foot. Wasn't any car."

"Fast runner, I guess."

"Something else. He removed the bulbs on my porch so there wouldn't be any light on him. At least, he unscrewed them to off. That way we couldn't see him run off."

"Was there any kind of noise out there? A sound of some sort?"

"He would have had to jump from the top step but I didn't hear any noise of him landing."

"Let me remind you, all of you, that I have a tape recorder going taking all this testimony down."

"Got nothing to hide or want to forget."

"Can you describe his face?"

"The man never came out of the shadows, outside or inside."

"Nobody else saw him?"

"The wife was in the kitchen. The rabbi was in the den. Just me and him!"

"How'd he sound?"

"Like brushing your teeth and gargling afterward, Raspy voice! Hoarse!"

"Clothes?"

"I think slacks, dark jacket. He stayed in the shadow. Never stepped into the light."

"Odor? Shaving lotion or something?"

"None. I shook his hand after he handed me the money. Like squeezing soft ice cubes."

"Tell me about the eyes again, Mr. LaVine."

"Tony, it was like you put a light inside his head and played a light to the outside through his eyes. Like a pumpkin!"

"I saw that too," added the rabbi.

"Couldn't have been a reflection from another site, could it?"

"Not from where I stood."

"How do you suppose Opfer is spelled?"

"No idea. I wrote that in my statement because that is how it sounded to me."

"Wonder why he screamed or whatever that sound was. What frightened him?"

"Seemed that it was my attire," offered the rabbi. "I had removed my shirt to show Murray a talisman I wear. He had pulled me into the foyer to thank the man for his donation. I expect a scantily clad rabbi startled him."

"I wonder! Is there a European superstition connected with that talisman?"

"I don't know of one. In Orthodox Jewry, it's worn as an undergarment, a sort of blessing token. I don't think the habit is prevalent anywhere much anymore. Maybe in Israel or Eastern Europe."

"You really think he had a European accent? I couldn't tell. I can't think of any origin I'd place him."

"From what you two tell me, the garment frightened him off!"

"It certainly had a negative effect on him. When I appeared, he howled an awful sound and really took off."

"Maybe he has a thing about you, Ira! I introduced Ira as a rabbi. Maybe he has a thing about rabbis."

"It's more than just a coincidence. I seem to be running into a series of things, bad things, all concerning and involving Jews. We have an ex-Nazi, a neo-Nazi, and his common law wife, All killed in horrible manners."

"Obviously related incidents."

"I don't know about that."

"So what do you think?"

"I don't know. If we have vengeful Jews running around like lunatics there could defiantly be a relationship."

[121]

"That sounds quite plausible. I'd like to help on the case if it will be okay with you and your superiors, Mister Pickett."

"At this point we need all the help we can get."

"Want to help too, Murray?"

"After last night you couldn't keep me away."

"Rabbi Silman, I wish I could get you together with a friend of mine who has some ideas about this situation. I personally think he's off his rocker with some of his thoughts, but your slant on what he says would interest me. I must warn you ahead of time that I really think he is nutty with some of those ideas of his."

"We apparently are both available and interested."

"I'll call him and see if he is available."

Tony's call was put through to José White by the hospital operator.

"Howdy do, Doc! Yeah! Busy as hell! I still think that. Listen! We had some queer events that have just occurred. Some may fit in with your nonsense. Can I bring a couple of interested folks over to your office so we can talk? Got time?"

Turning away from the phone, Tony whispered to the group behind him, "He's the pathologist at the hospital." He turned back to the phone. "Great! We're on our way!"

The three men got into the patrol car and Tony drove to the rear entrance of the island hospital. They entered and took an elevator to the third floor where the laboratory was located. José was waiting at the door to the lab and ushered the group back to his office. He had cleared the space for four chairs around a table in the office. It had meant rearranging two microscopes and piles of slides to another table. They were seated and Tony introduced the other two men to the doctor.

"Go ahead, Doc! Tell them the crazy stuff you told me when you worked over Annie Wilson."

"Stop prejudicing us, Mister Pickett."

"You are right, Mister President. I'll shut up."

"Go ahead, Dr. White!" urged the rabbi.

"Hear me all the way. My wife, Pam White, investigated these thoughts. We had a long discussion on the subject."

"She's something else, men! Ought to be in law enforcement on the island. Brainy broad!"

"That's why I married her!"

"Please go ahead with the 'nutty' part, Doctor White," begged the rabbi.

"Well, Pam and I got into a discussion on the subject of vampires, the Eastern European superstition! She pointed out how this could explain some of the questionable things that have been happening on the island."

"Hold on, Doctor! I am a layman and never got beyond a certain success in the dress business. I am not as educated as the rest of you. I am going to be a bit slower in swallowing what sounds like is coming. In this day and age, vampires?"

"Let the doctor finish, Murray," said the rabbi. "Then we'll discuss the possibilities."

"Stop and consider!" continued the doctor. "You read that some large animal is attacking live stock on the island. It's been in the 'Sound' several times. Three human victims have more or less been attacked and actually slaughtered as well. As if mutilated by a large animal. And blood has been drawn from all these victims. Victims of savagery."

"I can see what he is leading up to and I can't believe I am hearing things like this and sitting still."

"Do shut up, Murray!"

"But he's leading us to Dracula, Ira!"

"There's more, Mister LaVine. We're dealing with a thing that can go through locked doors, impossible to penetrate, No animal can accomplish that. No wolf! No wolf opens locked

[123]

doors or passes through them. So couldn't the animal and the man be one and the same?"

"Only in Hollywood! Or on television! Or comic books! I can't believe that intelligent people are having such a discussion!"

"I agree with the president here. But I have nothing else to go on, You got any other ideas?"

"Certainly not fictional mumbo jumbo!"

"Murray let him finish and then present your views."

José smiled at both men. "I can't blame you. I probably do sound as if I have gone crazy. All I'm doing is showing how such a creature could manage these horrors. Murders and impossible robberies! Nothing happening except after dark. And all the blood that is missing. Blood which these creatures need to survive!"

"A real fancy prepared dish!" muttered LaVine sarcastically.

"And now we have it disappearing from in front of your house so rapidly! Yes! Tony has called and told me about your experience. These things can vaporize and slip off into thin air. It fits!"

"So you're telling me I shook hands with a vampire?"

"I am just offering an explanation of what could have happened. It fits the chain of events that have occurred. Even if it does sound like science fiction."

Murray wiped his hands with his handkerchief. "Even if it ain't four in the afternoon, I need a drink!"

Rabbi Silman shook his head. "I could use one too. I have lived with spiritual things all my life. After all, religion is basically a mixture of superstitions. That concept I can accept. But supernatural I don't accept too easily. I teach there is a God. I don't tell my congregation what He looks like. Most picture an elderly, white haired individual sitting on a throne, looking down at us and judging! Orders are sent to scores of angels, who do the

[124]

carrying out of his orders. It adds a tone of credibility to the concept. But this! I just don't know!"

"Tell me, Mister LaVine! Did the thing show a reflection in a mirror?"

"How would I know? Who looks to see if somebody is reflecting in a mirror?"

White sat back and continued. "And the eyes are probably hypnotically used. Powerful agents! Fiction is usually based on some semblance to reality. This type has been handed down for centuries and enhanced upon regularly. There must have been some original basis of fact."

The rabbi leaned forward and addressed the doctor. "You sound as if you are a devotee of Bram Stoker. Has he been your only source for information?"

"No! Pam and I spent a whole day at the library on this. Outside of movie scenarios there isn't much available. Writers expand on root screen material. This all seems to have begun with a character named 'Vlad the Impaler'. He was a Slovic Prince or Romanian King early in European history; noted for brutality and the death of thousands."

"Let me look through my library and see what I can find," said the rabbi.

"Damn it, Ira. Are you swallowing this crap?"

"I am willing to listen, Murray. You should at least listen. Consider. You don't have to accept! Just consider. Where does one turn when a dilemma is unsolvable? That's the concept of how religion started. Out of desperation for explanations for the unexplained!"

"You put it well, Ira."

Pickett interrupted. "This would be a break in this stuff, however unbelievable! Crimes have been committed to get clothes and money. By someone possibly with a raspy voice and beady eyes."

[125]

Murray laughed. "But don't look for him until after dark."

"Has anyone thought about when all this started?" asked the rabbi.

"A period of the evil eye?" asked Murray.

"I think I know what the rabbi is leading up to," said Jose.

"It all post dates the disappearance of the coffin imported for the temple. Neither it or the body that was in it have ever been found."

"So?" asked Murray.

"It's shortly after the disappearance that an anti-Semite was murdered so horribly."

"That was our first locked door problem."

"Rabbi Ira Silman, are you postulating that our vampire is our Holocaust victim from Poland? One that I pushed to get? For our shrine! Is everyone in this room crazy? I can't believe what I am hearing! All intelligent men swallowing this fairytale stuff. I feel like I'm with Flo when she drinks too much!"

"Consider this, Murray. He comes here in a coffin. Dirt in it is from Treblinka. Him inside with the dirt. The coffin and the driver who picks it up disappear. The driver reappears in a hypnotic state and helps secrete the coffin. Fit so far?" the rabbi tried to explain.

"Pam figured out the driver was talking German," continued the doctor. "Remember, Tony? *Kauen Meister*! Chew master! *Kasette*! Coffin! These are German words and relate to what we are talking about. Mind you! Not Polish! I bet that accent is an oddball German one!"

"In mythical tales the vampire cannot abide a crucifix and is repelled by one." The rabbi offered this fact.

"That's the gimmick used in movies," said Tony. "And garlic!"

"So, how about an undergarment?"

[126]

"You mean we got us a Jewish vampire who is turned off by a shawl?" yelled the president of the temple.

"That could just be. A victim of the Nazis! My God! A Jewish vampire! A holy Jewish talisman! That's what spooked it, Murray! The shawl is on a rabbi yet!"

"So when Ira walks into my foyer like that, he takes one look, howls his head off, and runs away?"

"Are you wavering, Murray?"

"I am definitely tipping."

White continued. "The need for blood is covered by all of this. No matter the ethnic origin, these creatures need blood to survive. And they can fly. Like bats do! And I imagine they can turn into other animals as well."

"A dybbuk!" announced the rabbi.

"A who?" asked Tony.

"A dybbuk is a demon, not unlike a vampire, of Jewish mystical origin. It can enter another body and perform all sorts of horrors and take other forms. There is an exorcism ceremony to get rid of such things. It's like other Jewish myths. A golem is a Frankenstein type creature made from clay who commits evil like a dybbuk does."

"This is a formidable pair, Ira!"

"I know, Murray. I can see how Licht got his comeuppance. But why the others?"

"I can explain that," said José. "Jones was a known anti-Semite around town. A neo-Nazi!"

"I can vouch for that," said Murray. "Vandalized the temple and tried to get others to do it too."

"Why poor Annie Wilson?" asked Tony.

"She carried Joab's baby. Remember the missing uterus?"

"Ok! Now let me get this straight. You folks are telling me that I got to warn Jew haters to watch out. Do you realize what will happen when I go public with this stuff? I'd be out of a job in no time. How do I tell my staff to proceed? And how do I keep out of the loony lock-up? It all sounds good on paper and in the telling and talking stage, but man, I have to write reports! You know as well as I do that this is a bunch of crap and we'd never convince anybody else. What would the paper print and how do I tell the town council I am proceeding? Wearing shawls and carrying garlic or something? You guys do what you have to do. But if you step over any legal lines I am gonna have to come down on you. You come up with something worthwhile you come to me before you try anything. Do I make myself clear?"

"Understood," responded José. "Now, where do we begin?"

"The area we have to cover goes from the airport over the entire island. That's also the mainland remember," said Murray.

"Let me show you all something I worked out." José took some papers from his desk and the others gathered around him, except for Tony. He stood aloof, but listening. "Here is a map of the island. Here is where they found the truck. I think Rudy has become a slave of Opfer. He helped him get to the island. The thing helps Rudy escape and Rudy and he move things to the island, then Rudy dies. Not needed anymore. The coffin is in some deserted spot on this island. Probably a warehouse. Deserted structure of some kind."

"Not much left on the island in deserted structures," said Murray.

Tony spoke up. "Tell you what I'm gonna do. I'll give my staff a description of this joker with what we got. Maybe someone else has met a guy with a gargely voice and beady eyes. No confrontations, you hear? We got real bullets and will bring down this homicidal maniac our way. No stake in his heart or even silver bullets. Lead ones will do the trick."

"We certainly won't go it alone, Tony," said José.

"Just don't become a posse."

"I'll see that you get a daily report on what we have or don't have."

"First thing, Rabbi. I want you to get us a bunch of those shawls. I want one for Flo, too," said Murray.

"I'll get right to it. Some for your staff too, Tony?"

"Can't you see me telling them to wear these things and why?"

"I'll let you all know when I get them. I suggest we do very little until they come."

"I'll let you all know when we should get together again. It'll be after the shawls come in. Oh, and remember that Pam is included in all this."

The news of the death of Karl Licht and his notorious past was published not only in the local paper, but all over the state and nationally in time. Television broadcasts were devoted to the story. It brought journalists to the island in large numbers. Locals were interviewed despite the fact that most knew few details of the event. Some became "reliable resources" involuntarily and some were quoted nationally in news reports on television. The situation proved to be good for local businesses, particularly hotels, motels, and restaurants. The traffic on the island became unbearable in a short time.

The state Anti-Defamation League sent representatives to investigate how Karl Licht had managed to settle on Breakers View Island (or anywhere else) without knowledge of his Nazi past being exposed. His name had been a prominent one on the list of wanted war criminals after investigations had revealed his involvement in holocaust activities. It was a well known fact that many of the Hitlerian hierarchy had fled to Argentina after the end of World War Two in Europe, and many of these had been exposed and dealt with accordingly. Eichmann had been spirited to Israel to stand trial and later be executed for his crimes against

[129]

humanity. But many had escaped detection, Licht being among the elusive ones.

Frau Licht had gone into seclusion and refused to be interviewed and made no contacts with anyone outside. Her children left the island abruptly and refused interviews at their respective home cities. Eventually it was the decision of the public (through the media) that Licht had deserved what happened to him. Photographs of the now closed restaurant were shown on television along with sites on Breakers view Island that had nothing to do with the horrible murder. The Chamber Of Commerce was delighted by the turn of events, which introduced the existence of the barrier island resort to the public so inexpensively for the local businesses and so thoroughly via newspaper and television. Missing were souvenirs of the ghastly events such as wolves with bloody fangs wearing a Breakers View Island pennant. Although many expected that they too, would soon be a part of the publicity connected with the island.

The murders of Joab Jones and Annie Wilson did not get the attention that Licht's murder had received. Pickett could not understand why, but was happy that these two cases had been ignored by the press. The influx of visitors to the island had produced many new problems for the constabulary. The most prominent of these were auto mishaps, commonly known as "fender benders." There were the usual issues with alcohol consumption as well.

Rabbi Ira Silman had received a huge carton of shawls such as the one he wore under his shirt. It was his plan to distribute these to those involved in the investigation in which he was a partner. He expected, and received, much in the way of assistance from many involved with him in this. Tony and Archie had absolutely refused to don any such garment. To do so would give an air of credence to what they considered to be a ridiculous explanation of the events involved in the investigation. This was a modern, civilized city. Such nonsense about vampires was too silly to come under consideration in the investigation, and completely unacceptable. The police considered that there was a serial, maniacal killer out there, who was human and would eventually make the mistake that would betray him. They had a breakthrough with the stolen money and the supposed fact that it was a man they sought. Conventional bullets would be what were needed for his final downfall. Certainly wolves did not rob shops or use cash for their wants.

The investigation group of unofficial law enforcement people understood the terms under which Tony Pickett had allowed them to participate unofficially in the investigation. The group consisted of Rabbi Ira Silman, president of the island temple congregation Murray LaVine, Hospital Pathologist José White. The group also included José's wife Pam, who was a second, and occasionally a third grade teacher. Flo LaVine was a nonparticipant but had knowledge of the affair.

Pam and José were seated at their dinner table finishing their evening meal. They were sipping brandy and discussing the facts they had.

"You think Opfer would cast a reflection in a mirror? Would exposure to sunlight cause his demise? And what do we do if we find this coffin? He obviously isn't going to be turned away by a crucifix. Do we strip to our underwear with these things to defend ourselves? Do you think garlic is effective?" Pam had accepted the fact that they were dealing with a vampire and needed assurance that they knew how to conquer it.

Her husband, trained in more scientific ways, was somewhat confused by the facts that had accumulated and was not quite ready to accept theories he himself had come up with in the case at hand.

"We both agree that there is something sort of supernatural here. That's plain to me anyhow. There's too much to think

[131]

otherwise. Using the term 'supernatural' can cover a lot of territory."

"Mention this to your colleagues at the hospital and you'll be drummed out of the corps."

"That's for sure. And do not mention this to any of the press hanging around."

"Boy would that make a headline!"

"Pam, suppose we catch up with this thing, this dybbuk, what do we do?"

"I imagine it sleeps all day and only functions at night after sunset, in the dark. All that has happened has happened at night. The rabbi thinks the creature was gassed to death and taken out of that mass grave in Poland! If he intends to wreck vengeance on everybody that's still around that contributed to the holocaust, maybe we should let him be. Good way to combat anti-Semitism. Remove the suckers!"

"But what happens when he runs out of culprits? Annie wasn't involved with the other two. What happens when the cows are gone and there are no more Jew haters in these parts?"

"I guess he moves on to other territories."

"And hits innocents like Annie? We can't allow him to move on."

"Mama Licht and her offspring ought to be on the lookout these days."

"And any grandchildren! Do you see the ramifications?"

The phone rang and it was answered by José.

"Who was that?"

"The rabbi! He talked Tony and Hay into wearing a shawl."

"That'll upset the Baptist Church!"

"They think the idea is nutty but are getting a little nervous."

"Love to get a photo of them in the shawl."

"We need Pickett and Hay."

"Bet those shawls don't get washed every night or morning."

The next morning in his office, José was informed that Singleton had died. The cause was given as heart failure. The three, José, Tony, and Archie, sat in at the autopsy report and discussion.

On the way back to the island, Hay expounded, "Witches! Vampires! All this loony material! A month ago I suggested you all be put in the nut house. Now I'm not sure what I think. Just can't accept all this bullshit."

"So fifty years ago how would men have responded to a man walking on the moon with a golf stick?"

"I see your point! Let me ask you a question! And if you tell anyone I asked, I'll deny it."

"What?"

"I been reading about this shit. Doesn't anyone who gets bit by these things turn into one himself?"

"Another vampire! That's what the man who wrote *Dracula* would have us believe."

"So we can expect visits from Licht, Joab, Annie, Rudy, and more wolves?"

"I expect it is the way the blood is removed has something to do with that."

"So we could use the victims to get to the big guy?"

"True! At least it ought to be true."

"And if Rudy was helping the big guy and the others weren't?"

"I see your point. He wouldn't use anti-Semites as helpers."

"And we figure the big guy is who killed Rudy. Not a heart attack!"

"And he didn't remove all his blood either."

"And didn't gash out his throat."

Tony spoke. "Seems he wasn't so grateful to Rudy for his help."

"That's the point, Tony. He didn't mutilate Rudy."

[133]

"Geez, Doc! You think he's gonna bring Rudy back to help some more?"

"Looks that way to me, Archie."

"So what do we do now? Put a watch on Rudy's grave? Make sure he's in the damn thing?"

"I'd say so! I have no idea of the time element involved in such things. Don't even know if it's necessary."

"You know what, Doc? This shit sounds like a movie. Now I am cast as an actor in it. If Rudy is gonna start eatin' cows, guess who's gonna get the job of makin' sure it's him. Can't tell the rest of the staff about this. I suppose we should be watching all the anti-Jews in the area."

"If I assign a grave watch on you, make sure you wear that scarf thing," said Tony.

"Don't make funnies! Only thing around my neck will be a cartridge belt and a cross I got from a babe I know. Don't want to confuse Gods involved here. My gun will be my savior!"

"My wife and I have the same God, Archie. We wear this shawl and the crucifix day and night!"

""Play it safe both ways, Doc?"

Back at the headquarters building, the three men discussed the plans for the grave watch. Rudy had been buried in a Baptist cemetery just off the island. No family had shown up for the burial. Only Tony, Pam, and José had been there. Pam wanted to join the men in the watch, but was forbidden to do so. It would be Archie and Jose the first night. Tony and another deputy would take over the second and the deputy would be ordered to wear a shawl.

"Make that really black coffee, Pam."

She was filling two thermoses. "Black's the only kind I make, buster!"

"Very funny."

"Wear that scarf all night and yank it out in the open if you have to."

"Apparently there's an aura about it. I doubt it has to be out in the open, just worn!"

"You going to stay all night?"

"Tony is going to spell us in about five or six hours. I may hang on there after Archie leaves out of anxiety."

"They wearing the things?"

"Tony is. Archie is pretty stubborn. He's been ordered to, but I doubt he'll obey."

"He may be sorry."

"Some girlfriend of his gave him a crucifix. He's gonna trust that!"

"Hope to God both of the things work!"

"In a way, I do too. Will give us a line on this dybbuk thing."

"You really think Opfer will show?"

"I have no idea what to expect. In all probability, we'll freeze our asses off and nothing will occur."

"Suppose this Rudy person does get up and walk about. He wasn't Jewish and this shawl thing isn't going to bother him. Probably never even met a Jew in his lifetime."

"Why be half safe? We got crosses too. Cover both ends!"

"What if nothing happens?"

"Probably give it another night or two. Then we'll know the thing can't pass it on, or maybe doesn't want to."

"The other three didn't come back."

"They seemed to have died differently."

"Oh! I meant to tell you."

"What?"

"Remember that letter you got from your European buddy? The one who told us about the mass grave stuff?"

"What about it?"

"The grave was in Poland, but the victim was German. So I got my German dictionary. This poor soul was apparently one of the Jews of Hitler's massacres. You know what '*Opfer*' means in English?"

"I'm positive you are going to tell me."

"'*Opfer*' in German means 'victim!'"

The patrol car drove slowly as it left the island, heading for the cemetery not more than two or three miles away. It was cloudy, almost bordering on a rainy one. At five in the afternoon, it seemed as though evening was arriving. The rush hour of cars leaving the island had been in session for an hour and a half. The congestion was usually caused by a traffic light about half a mile off the island.

"After watching some of that autopsy, we can both be pretty sure this guy is dead. Christ, Doc, what do they do with all them parts in them jars?"

"That's a good question, Arch! I have a ton of those jars on shelves. I don't know! If something comes up about the cause of death or some legal thing is involved, you often need those tissues handy."

"Autopsies bother me a lot. How does anyone know the guy don't feel what's going on?"

"Nobody has ever complained about that as far as I know!"

"And neither will this joker. This has got to be one of the stupidest assignments I ever got. Pickett, of all people! I know he don't go along with this vampire shit! Can't figure out what's got into him lately. You folks are all highly educated people. How can you even consider this stuff?"

"I will admit that one has to stretch his imagination to swallow a lot of what we've been talking about. Under any normal circumstances I'd consider the ideas crazy. But too much fits here. Elsewhere, I would think a lot of hogwash if I read

[136]

about it in the newspaper. But I've been in on some of this stuff and some pieces of the puzzle do fit. Really reads like a novel, doesn't it? Or some movie script!"

"It took you a lot of schooling to get where you are, Doc. With all that time at books and stuff, watching you involve yourself in this amazes me. And Mrs. White is a smart lady, and she's into this crap too!"

"Frankly, Arch, I hope to hell you are right. And it is a lot of just that. Crap! But unfortunately we feel obligated to follow up on these superstitions and suspicions."

"Ah, Doc! Nothin's gonna happen! You'll see! We're gonna feel real stupid doin' what we're doin'."

"I really hope you are right."

"You really can't think Rudy is gonna dig himself outta the ground where he's buried. That, with half his insides in a jar back in the county building sitting on a shelf. How's he gonna eat anything? Fall right through what is left of him."

"You'd better be right about that part. We are going to be in real hot water if he can grow them back again!"

"He does, and I invest in the company that makes those scarves you guys wear."

"You should be wearing one, Arch! What's the harm?"

"I think wearing one is the silliest part of all this nonsense crap! I got a gun in a holster at my side to protect me from whatever might, and note I said might, attack us. Next thing you know, we'll be told to have a crucifix handy and wear garlic around our necks! How far they gonna go with this shit?"

"To tell you the truth, I don't have the garlic, but I do have those other things on me! Covering all the bases."

"Why be half safe, right, Doc?"

"Got all the possibilities covered."

"Gonna be brisk out tonight. Only that scarf is gonna keep you warmer than me."

The driver, another deputy, pulled the patrol car into the gateway that led onto a short drive into the cemetery. It was about eight miles from the causeway that led to Breakers View Island. The causeway went over the Inland Waterway, which is what made an island out of the land. The waterway went north to enter a sound on the east coast of the island. Another large sound was on the west side. The Atlantic Ocean formed the border on the south end of the island.

The car stopped at a small rectangular building at the beginning of the grave area of the place. It was a brown building with no surrounding landscaping. The driver and the two passengers got out of the car and walked to the door of the small building. It was opened by an elderly, Black male. He was dressed in denim clothing, and wearing a thick, black sweater.

"You the gents gonna greet out latest guest when he wakes up?"

José suddenly felt a bit of panic. How much had this man been told of the affair? And how much had he told others? If the public got wind of this there'd be hell to pay. And the media would have a ball with the facts. They, themselves, would be laughing stocks and who could blame anyone that thought so.

"What do they call you?" asked Archie Hay.

"Eldridge Edison. Sir! Been watchin' over these quiet folks for about four years now. They ain't no bother. Easy job! All sleepers! Nobody ever got up for a stroll I know of. No walkin' and no talkin'."

"Well Mister Edison, we are here to make sure that don't happen."

"Ain't seen grave sitters before! You ain't gonna be upset I don't sit out here with you fellers? Gonna be a cool one tonight. Besides I sure would feel like horse's ass makin' sure nobody got up in a cemetery."

[138]

"No problem, Mister Edison! Stay here with him, Frank!" Archie addressed the other deputy, who had driven them to the place. "Stay by the radio. Anything you think we should know, come out and tell us. I got my phone and pager too with me. But if Tony calls in, let me know. He said he'd call in just before he comes out to spell us later. Hope to hell he's on time."

José put on the jacket he'd brought with him.

"No heaters out there, gents. Nobody seems to mind how cold it gets. Never had a single complaint."

"Very funny, Eldridge! Now show us where this latest grave is located."

The graveyard was shaped like a pentagon and they were led to the farthest corner from the gatehouse. It was about a hundred and fifty yards into the grave area. It had become darker by then. There was no moonlight.

The freshly dug grave was designated by a mound of dirt seven feet long and about three and a half feet wide. There were no adornments, flowers, or a marker to denote that there was an occupant. A small sign lay on the ground to one side with a name and a date of burial and a number. José picked it up and planted it to the side of the grave. This was the only indication that Rudy singleton's final resting place was here.

"Not much to show for having been alive once. Even for a short lifetime, Doc."

"Doubt he gives a damn, Arch!"

"Goddamn! We are gonna freeze our asses off sittin' here. Lucky it's cold as it is or the bugs be bitin' mounds in us. No good reason for this shit. I make overtime but you get zip, Doc! You're nuts, you ask me!"

"Can't disagree much!"

"Sure ain't gonna tell anyone about this assignment. Word got out would make 'em laugh me off the face of the earth."

"I sure won't tell a soul!"

[139]

Archie held up a rifle he carried and pointed to the holster at his side. "Nothin' gonna get by me with these babies along!"

"Look very formidable!"

"Won't miss at this distance. Never shot a wolf!"

"We need light. I'll hold the flashlight!"

"Hope to hell Tony's on time. Let him bust his ass freezin' out here. Serve him right!"

For the next three hours the two men sat pretty much in silence except for short remarks every fifteen or twenty minutes.

"Don't take offence, Doc, if I ask you a question?"

"What do you want to know, Arch?"

"You ever have trouble down here in the South? I mean with your wife bein' what she is?"

"I'd be lying if I denied it. It's funny though! I expected things be a lot worse than they are now. We had some troubles along the way, but they were up North. Amazing! Actually, the worst part was dealing with her family and the Blacks in Africa!"

"You got a beautiful woman there. I feel uncomfortable talkin' with her."

"Why would you feel that way?"

"She's so smart! Makes me feel dumber than I am. She's using words I never even heard before and I know damn well they are good English words."

José laughed. "That's what graduate schooling does for you. You've been in school as long as she has you'd be using those words too. You been educated as long as she has, color will make no difference."

Another forty minutes of silence ensued. It was suddenly broken by a wailing sound that came from the wooded area about a mile behind that portion of the cemetery where the two men were stationed, and they both arose at once.

"What the hell was that?"

[140]

"Sounded like a coyote howling, Archie!"

"No such around these parts, Doc!"

The sound was repeated, only closer this time.

"Put out that cigarette, Arch."

The two got into kneeling positions. Archie put the gun into his arm bend and waited.

"I have the flash ready. I won't turn it on unless something is there to light up. I am aiming it at the grave itself though." They both spoke in loud whispers.

"Any wolf shows up he's gonna get six thirty-eight slugs and then I'll empty the rifle into him."

"Hope they work! Don't fire too soon. Wait until I nudge you. He should enter this grave, so let's move back a little."

They backed up about ten to twenty yards and kept watching the copse. Suddenly sounds emanated from the copse. It was slightly after midnight now and very dark. José felt no fear, strangely enough, just a surge of excitement. He became aware of the silence everywhere else in the area.

"Christ Doc! Look at that!"

From the edge of the mound of earth in the center of Singleton's grave, a thick vapor arose, as if from a kettle of boiling water. It swirled in a spiral fashion and grew denser and denser, coalescing into a solid shape neither man could identify.

Archie Hay rose up with pistol in one hand and rifle in the other. "Come on you bastard! I'm ready for you. Show yourself. Come out. Come on!" He ran directly toward the grave.

"Archie! For God's sakes! Stop! Come back and stay away from that thing!" yelled José, half screaming.

"Bullshit!"

"Don't be a damn fool. Come back!"

Gonna clear this up once and for all, Doc!"

He moved steadily toward the grave. The vapor had disappeared and in its place stood what appeared to be a figure of what José supposed to be Rudy Singleton. Recognition of Rudy stopped Archie's advance momentarily.

"Don't go near the thing." screamed José.

Hay emptied his revolver and got even closer, then raised the rifle to fire while walking steadily towards the figure. "You ain't real. You can't be! Die you son-of-a-bitch!" He pulled the rifles trigger repeatedly. He was close enough now to touch the apparition.

"Hay! You damn fool. Damn you! Come back!" He pulled the shawl from under his shirt and began to wave it in the air as he advanced.

The thing that had been Rudy Singleton reached out and grabbed Archie before the excited officer could use the rifle as a club. Its hand clawed Archie's throat and tore away the front of his neck. Archie tried to scream but made nothing but a gurgling sound and went limp in the creatures grasp. The thing then leaned over toward the gash in the neck and began to drink the blood that was squirting from the wound.

"This better work! I love you Pam!" shouted José as he ran toward the horror site waving the shawl in the creature's face. It let out a howl and disappeared as a cloud of vapor. The vapor then rolling out across the cemetery toward the wooded area behind the graves. Another howl came from the distant copse as though another wolf was seeking his mate.

"What's going on?" yelled the deputy, arriving on the scene in a run. I heard shots and screams."

"Here! Give me a hand!" yelled José. Together they turned over Archie's body.

"Oh my God! Archie!" yelled the deputy.

"Get on that radio and get Pickett out here. He's to bring the crew he uses for things like this, and most important, he's to bring Rabbi Silman from the temple out here now."

Eldridge Edison stood staring, behind the vomiting deputy.

[142]

"Who does the digging here, Edison?" asked José.

"A team with a tractor. It's parked over there."

"Call them and get them out here as soon as possible. Tell them we want this grave opened as soon as they can. Tell them it's that or spend the night in jail for refusing."

It was about thirty minutes before José heard the approaching sirens. He'd been afraid that the creature might arise and finish dinner. Having been Baptist, Rudy might not pay attention to the shawl again. Luckily, Rudy had been a slave product of a Jewish master. The shawl had worked.

The ambulance arrived first. It was followed by three patrol cars and a pickup truck. The flashing lights with intermittent splotches of red gave an eerie appearance to the scene. It was still cold enough to prohibit the usual symphonic sounds of the insect population. The sky had changed as well. The cloud cover suddenly lifted exposing the beacon-like appearance of the moon that illuminated the scene below. A slight breeze came from the north, adding to the briskness of the temperature.

Tony Pickett jumped from the first of the patrol cars to arrive and ran to the rear of the cemetery to the scene of the horror there. He was followed by seven other members of his staff, all with flashlights beaming. The ambulance crew carried a stretcher.

Rabbi Ira Silman had accompanied Pickett to the place but did not run back with the others, knowing he would not be able to alter anything with his presence. He pulled his shawl out from under his shirt as he walked to the scene of activity, and let it protrude from his jacket.

"Oh Jesus! Archie!" Tony knelt by the inert figure of his deputy and friend. "Oh my god!" he held his hand over his face as he knelt and began to sob aloud. After a few minutes, he arose and began to give orders to the people around him.

[143]

Photographers recorded every section of the site with flashes lighting up the area like an exploding was scene. Other deputies explored the entire area, picking up anything that looked like it did not belong in the cemetery and placing it in plastic bags. Flashlights shone all over the area for an hour after the arrival of the deputies. Hay's body was placed in a dark body bag and carried to the ambulance on the stretcher that had been brought by the ambulance crew.

"Tell me exactly what happened, Doc! Don't leave out anything, no matter how insignificant it sounds." Tony sat on the ground near the grave of Rudy Singleton. "Get this guy out of here!" He referred to Edison, who stood by the deputies and just stared at the scene open mouthed and obviously frightened by all the activity. He was sent back to the building at the entrance to the cemetery where he was questioned by a deputy seeking to know what he had seen and observed.

"Perhaps we should question the doctor in private, Mister Pickett," said the rabbi. "These other people might find the facts a bit weird, don't you think?"

"Your right! Let's go sit in my car, Doctor White, and talk." Tony gave orders to the rest of the attendees and he, the rabbi and the doctor got into his patrol car; the doctor and Tony in front and the rabbi in the back.

"I'm gonna tape this," said Tony, setting up a small recorder which he placed on the seat between them. "Go ahead from the beginning."

"Now, you two listen carefully to what I have to say. I am going to start with our arrival here tonight at the gatehouse. The deputy that drove Archie and me did not witness the events later, which was lucky I think. It was unbelievable, but what I tell you is going to be exactly as I witnessed. I won't leave out anything. Every detail!"

It was a lengthy, gory, detailed description.

[144]

"You have to be with us now, Tony!" the doctor finished relating the evening's events and Tony turned off the recorder.

"I do and I am now! God damn! It's really science fiction. One of them B movies."

"Now will you start wearing one of these things?" The rabbi passed a shawl to Tony.

"I sure will. Definitely! But I am going to have to work on this solo. Can't give any of this to the rest of the department. Let them think it was an animal! Archie gone, I'll work this alone."

Tony removed his shirt and the rabbi showed him how to don the fringed garment with the fringes hanging down the front and in the back as it slipped over his head. "I have more of these if anyone needs one. Apparently they do work, from what the good doctor tells us. Must wear one at all times now."

"Not gonna bring in any of my men on this. They ain't gonna believe any of this shit anyhow!"

"No! You are right. We must act alone now. The news must not get out to the rest of the island."

"So the bastard is really out there someplace."

"I never did get a good look at him, or whatever it was out there. The howling came from way back in the wooded area where he disappeared into.

"He'll be back before daylight. We have to wait!"

A small truck arrived at the gatehouse. José went over to the two men who got out of the truck. He detailed what they were to do.

"When you get it up, leave it alongside the hole and go home. The chief here will call you in the morning about reburying the thing. Please work as fast as you can now in getting it up."

"You know Sir; you really need a court order to do this. This is against the law."

"The Chief there is taking all the responsibility. This is a major emergency and a secret government activity!"

[145]

The two men went over and started a small tractor and drove it to the grave area at the back.

"Good thing you sent Edison home for the night, Tony."

"Told him the police would watch the place tonight. A day timer arrives in the morning. We ought to be through by then."

Tony checked his weapon to be sure it was ready for any necessity. The backhoe machine began digging down to the coffin. It took about forty minutes to expose the coffin. Two huge chains were passed under it with a drill like machine and it was raised up and placed on the side of the hole in the ground. "Thanks men. I'll call you in the morning to put it back down. This is government hush-hush stuff! Remember that! Not a word to anybody or you yourselves will be in big trouble. Do I make myself clear?"

The men left without saying anything more.

"So now what?" asked Tony.

"We wait! He's got to come back before dawn!"

The rabbi took out a small book from his jacket pocket. "This must be done tonight or someone will suffer like Archie. We have to decapitate and the burn the body. I have read dybbuk literature. These are incantations they say over the creature. It's an Eastern European Yiddish exorcism ritual. The important thing is the beheading."

"I'll handle that. I brought a dissection kit from the lab for that, Rabbi!"

"Something like being at home in the office, eh Doc?"

"Ghastly business!" said the rabbi.

"Well, seeing is believing. Can't doubt what the Doc has seen. Is this thing out there looking for more supper? And where the hell is the big guy? Where's he been in all this shit?"

"I wish I knew!" said José. "I don't know if they go out every night or once a week or what!"

[146]

"My reading does not tell me how long these things go on. I don't think they live forever. These legends have existed for centuries and events around them have probably been altered to fit crimes that have occurred. There's no set pattern to these tales. Stoker embellished on Gypsy lore from Eastern Europe. His story has things that certainly do not fit this pattern of events. Most of the vampire facts are based in the imaginations of novelists and screenwriters. The one factor I see in common to all is the beheading. I have no idea if cremation is essential."

"Spooky stuff. So this shawl thing really worked, Doc?"

"Disappeared in a puff of smoke! Howled in anger too! Like a banshee!"

"Never heard a banshee!"

"It's a howler! A female howler! Howls when her love is going to expire. Irish legend."

"Did whatever this was, Rudy, or whatever, speak or say anything out loud?" asked the rabbi.

"Nope! Just sounded like an angry animal."

"There's that wolf thing again. Like that print we found at Licht's restaurant. That was a wolf or an awfully big dog."

"No dog unlocks doors. The vapor thing seems to cover the getting in and out."

"Guess as the only witness I gotta put a watch on you, Doc."

"I've thought about that, Tony. Pam and I will keep these shawls on at all times. Don't think for a minute that I wan't scared. Thank God it worked!"

"Taking care of Rudy or whatever it is he's become will cue us in on what to do about Opfer if we ever find him. He may create other aides if given time. That will be a catastrophe."

Tony looked to the east. "Hey! It's getting light. If something does happen it better happen soon."

The three men stepped back from the coffin now to about twenty yards away. The moon was covered again by a grouping of clouds. All was still. José noticed that the noise of the insects which had begun an hour earlier suddenly stopped.

[147]

Rabbi Silman rubbed his forehead and realized that despite the brisk temperatures he was sweating. José was somewhat frightened now. Tony was experiencing a sense of exhilaration rather than fright.

"Holy shit! Look at that!" whispered Pickett. He pointed toward the edge of the wood copse. A shadowy figure was racing toward the cemetery. Tony drew his gun from its holster.

The thing resembled a large wolf. It jumped the fence at the rear of the cemetery and approached the coffin that sat above the ground and stopped. It seemed puzzled by the coffin being where it was. It suddenly disappeared and in its place was a thick winding vapor spiraling in the air. The vapor was sucked somehow into the coffin.

No one spoke. The three men watched as daylight came and bathed them in sunlight.

"Easy! Give it time, Rabbi!" José was not too eager to get near the coffin.

"I feel like I'm dreaming this and not fully awake," whispered Tony. "If Rudy is inside that thing, I definitely will need no more convincing."

"Pam could handle this better than I can," said José.

"Without seeing it, the president of my congregation could not handle this either."

They sat and waited for another half hour. Finally Tony walked up to the coffin. He undid the clasps on the lid. "Have them scarves ready, and if I say so, run like hell from here."

The lid was opened. Rudy Singleton lay in the coffin, appearing peacefully asleep. His jeans in which he was buried did not appear dirty, and the body did not appear to be caved in despite the fact that the innards were in a jar miles away. He appeared to be just a young man resting peacefully.

After overcoming the initial shock of the scene, José went to work. He took instruments from the kit he'd brought along for this purpose and proceeded to remove the head. The rabbi watched with horrified fascination at the decapitation. Tony gagged a bit.

"Now let's get this coffin reburied. I'll get those guys back here for that." He closed the lid of the coffin. "I'll take you and this back to the island and come back for the reburial. Then I'm gonna burn this thing up someplace where nobody can watch."

"Be sure they don't open it when they come to rebury it!"

"No problem. I'll be here! And I know just the spot to burn this thing I got in this bag. I'm gonna burn it down to the last bit. Will scatter the ashes and nobody will ever discover anything of Rudy Singleton's head."

Fingering the shawls they wore, the three men got in the county car and left the area.

"Never had this for breakfast before, Mrs. Silman," said Pam. "I've eaten these things at other times, but never for breakfast."

"Please call me Hedy. Like the movie queen, only I never ran through the woods naked."

"I saw that movie a long time ago. It's been rerun on TV many times and I watch it whenever I see it's gonna be on." Tony chewed and spoke at the same time. "Man, she was a beauty! When I was a kid you had to be eighteen to see it."

"Well, I'm no Hedy type. My real name is Hedva but nobody's called me that since I was a little girl. So what do they have for breakfast in Kenya, Pam?"

"Certainly not herring and lox! We eat *biringani, embe, maji ya matunda, machunga, and ndiziiz!*"

"You know I need a translation!" laughed the rabbi.

"Basically, it's fruit, eggplant, and juices."

"Was that Swahili?"

"When we have an argument, that's all I get," added José. "It helps because she suddenly realizes that I have no idea what she's angry about!"

"Well I've had toasted bagels but never smoked fish in the morning. And raw onions at this hour. I'd have to gargle before getting to the kids at school. Teachers have to be careful that way. Like dentists!"

"Not to worry, Pam. These are Vidalia. Publicity says they are sweet and leave nothing on the breath. How about you, doctor? You ever eat this sort of thing for breakfast?"

"The fish? And hard boiled eggs and raw vegetables? Nope! The fruit, yes. Spanish goes with the fruit and often vegetables, but not smoked fish. May I ask Pam for this from now on?"

"Listen, sucker! Know what this stuff costs? This one, not the salmon!"

"That's a chub, Pam. It's smoked whitefish! Try it with lemon squeezed on it."

"Listen, Hedy! You could get our monster out in the open with temptations like this. Should taste better than what he's been eating so far," added Hedy's husband.

The statement produced a moment of silence around the table.

"He doesn't seem to like conventional food, Ira. Maybe we should stir in some beets and red cabbage," said José, breaking the silence.

"We got to do something real soon," said Tony. The town fathers are comin' down on me real hard. What happened to Archie really blew things apart. Mayor calls every day now. They want us to get outside help. If they get it, then you know the problems we are gonna have. How do I explain what we know to be factual? And what's the press gonna do with that?"

"What have you given out?"

"That Archie was attacked by a large animal, a wolf, or a pack of feral dogs. Shelter is full of them. No room for more, so they run wild. People from the mainland dump unwanted dogs and cats on the island. We've caught some in the act! But we can't get 'em all! These mutts forage all over the island for food. Gang up at night into packs and you can spot them in the back of restaurants and supermarkets."

"Damn shame!" muttered Pam.

"How do they deal with this sort of thing in Kenya?"

"Well Hedy, if there is a drought then there's a problem. People eat dogs. If they're pushed out of the house then it's the same thing as here. Larger animals hunt and eat them. Particularly the hyenas!"

"Some wise guy is gonna realize the similarity and there's gonna be a shooting gallery here. And then I got to chase after the hunters."

[150]

"Tony is right. He has a big problem. There's nobody going to accept the facts as we know them," said the rabbi. "Superstitions are never translated into reality these days. Who is going to believe that we have a vampire in our midst? Who even knows what a dybbuk is or accepts the existence of werewolves?"

"Look folks! I'm just a redneck cop in the South! No way I'm gonna be able to convince anybody that what I seen with my own two eyes was real. How would I put it? That a guy got up from his grave and ripped my best deputy apart and turned himself into a puff of smoke?"

"Which is exactly what the sucker did. Okay folks! Where do we go from here? The wolf thing has hit the public, or at least the big animal thing. I herd kids on busses every day. If the parents get panicky about the situation it'll be an awful mess. It will be the end of after school activities; no stragglers allowed. The parents are going to demand immediate action!"

"If I give out a description of a man like the one LaVine met at his house, what do I say? He's got a raspy voice. Looks like what?"

"I remember that night well. When I entered the foyer I saw nobody. Not in any mirror or lit area. I thought at the time I was at the wrong angle."

"I recall the movie *Dracula*! VanHelsing confronts Bela with a mirror and a crucifix," said José White. "Really upsets the villain."

"Well, we better get a legitimate sighting soon or I will be out of a job. I can't head off the outside help thing much longer. I have told the press that the danger seems to be after dark."

"I am amazed that nobody has come up with the Bram Stoker similarities yet," exclaimed José. "These folks are mostly Northern retirees and should be analyzing things soon along the '*Dracula* lines.'"

"He hasn't got Rudy to help him anymore. He has to move that coffin around by himself," said Pam.

"I can tell you one thing. I am frightened! For my husband! Ira has been very close in this thing. If he needs help, he can create a stable of zombies. What if he decides to move off the

[151]

island? Who's to stop him? Imagine this sort of thing in the middle of Florida or any other state for that matter!"

The rabbi hushed his wife. "Let's not get carried away by panic. What Hedy says is a possibility! He only functions after sundown. His life is restricted a good bit. He needs blood of apparently anything to keep going. We have a weapon in this shawl. And things have happened that show that it works. The good doctor here proved that when things happened with Rudy. We are dealing with a Jewish demon. I contacted Poland hoping that the authorities photographed the body before shipping it. Haven't had a reply yet. If they did, it may help to establish an identity. There may be other ways to fight this thing so I do not believe we are entirely helpless."

"Now he ain't living in any established residence in any coffin," said Tony. The absentee owners could arrive unexpectedly. So it has to be some empty warehouse or something. Been checkin' some rental outfits but I gotta be careful what I ask. We do have other tasks you know. Lotsa' accidents and break-ins and such. And I can't let the rest of my staff in on too much either. Acting alone! Takes time, folks!"

"He has to hole up someplace during the day," said Pam.

"I still have a problem in explaining what happened to Archie to my staff. We are supposed to be looking for a loony that drinks cow's blood and is strong as hell; that has to have been wounded at least by Archie's firing. And there's no way I can get these scarves on them without creating a real panic by explaining why."

The phone rang. "For you, Tony," said the rabbi.

After a muffled conversation with whoever was at the other end of the line, Tony hung up and turned to the group.

"I think we've got our first break, folks. That was a lady who works at Happy Timeout Rentals. They rent small condos and such. What timing! She doesn't know what happened to a co-worker. She rented a place to a guy with a raspy voice and funny eyes. That describes our guy!"

"That's how Murray described Opfer!" said the rabbi.

"Anyhow, the co-worker did not come into work the next morning and they can't get her to answer her phone."

[152]

"They have her address?"

"Too bad its Sunday! She won't be back at work until tomorrow if she does come back. That girl could be in big trouble! You should try and get to her today, Tony!"

"Yeah! I'll check her out. You know that the president of your congregation could be in trouble too. And his wife!"

"I'll call Murray right after you leave. They should be sure to wear the shawls all day and night. I'll update him on our talking this morning."

"Now I think if it, Tony. Hurry! That girl may be able to tell us where the thing has settled down," yelled Pam to the departing policeman.

The next morning was a wet one. Usually, at that time of the year, rainfall was light and lasted a short time. But this one was heavy with cyclone conditions. Two and a half inches fell in less than one hour and driving was extremely difficult. Tony parked in front of the small building and ran to the front door. When he opened the door, the odor informed him that he was going to have troubles today. A short, chubby woman came from the rear of the bungalow-like cottage wearing an apron over slacks. She had a huge kerchief covering her hair which was tied back into a bun.

"Sorry! We aren't open today. Had a fire last night. If you'll give me your number, we'll call you later this afternoon."

"I'm with the police, Ma'am!" He flashed his wallet badge. "I'm looking for a Miss Bunny Hardy!"

"That's me, Officer."

"Been to five offices this morning. Something tells me that this is the one I want."

"Come on back here and see what happened! All our records are gone. Somebody spilled gas or something into every drawer, onto both computers, and onto all the shelves and burned up everything in sight. Not a single record left! We have to make a public appeal for renters to come in voluntarily. Ain't no way to track down the rentals that are left here. Add the firemen pouring water onto everything. Unless people are honest to come in, we

[153]

don't collect rent from anyone. Take a month or two to check all over for them."

"You got a fat chance of people volunteering to pay. You folks handle commercial rentals too?"

"Nope. Only residential."

"You the only employee here?"

"I got an assistant."

"Can I talk to her? Where is she?"

"That's what I'd like to know. Never showed up to work yesterday. Tried to get her on the phone. No answer!"

"I have to speak to her!"

"You think she done this?"

"It's possible! Was she upset with the company? Unhappy about anything?"

"Not that I know of. Here's the boss's number. He can tell you where she lives."

Tony drove to the address on the card she'd given him. There he obtained the address of the missing employee. The Artisto Development Company had four or five rental offices scattered over the island. Tony phoned José White at the hospital. He was sure what he would find at the address given him.

"José! I'm on my way to Seven Oaks apartments. About three miles over the causeway. On the mainland! Meet me at number sixteen as soon as you can. Don't want to call a staff deputy for this!"

"Smart move! On my way!"

Pickett pulled up in front of unit sixteen and waited in the car. The rain did not let up as he sat there. He noticed an old ford coupe parked in the slot indicated for number sixteen. Twenty five minutes later José arrived and parked behind Tony. With an umbrella he knocked on the chief's car and Tony got out. It was important to have José there. He might have to pronounce someone dead.

"There was arson at the rental outfit."

"Bet I know the results! No records of the rentals left."

"No taker on that bet! No way to know where the rentals were located."

"Our boy is cleaver! Is this where you got that call from yesterday?"

"Nope! But I think this is where the gal that rented to our friend lives. She didn't show up for work yesterday, and Sunday is a busy day for them. No answer to her phone calls. That's her vehicle parked over in slot sixteen. The gal at the office works in the rear and this one handles the renting. I think she's in deep shit, Doc!"

"One way to find out!"

Tony rang the bell to the apartment. It was a small, one level, villa.'"Miz Sutton! Police! Mae Sutton!"

He knocked several times and there was no response.

"So now what, Tony?"

"Got the legal papers right here to do what we're gonna do next."

He took a passkey from his pocket. "Got this from her boss at Aristo."

Even though the key unlocked the door, they discovered the chain lock still fastened.

"I'm an old hand at these, José!" Tony took a wire from his pocket and maneuvered it about the chain bolt for several minutes and the door opened all the way. "Name is Mae Sutton! Worked in the front room. Bunny is a short fatty; works in the back room. Figure what we're gonna find in here ain't gonna be nice, Doc!"

"If she was in on the rental to our friend and someone destroyed those records then it doesn't look good!"

They were in a combination foyer and living room, adjoining a small kitchen.

"Keeps a neat place!" Tony walked to shut the door on the left side of the room. He inhaled deeply, exhaled, and opened the door. The unmade bed was the only thing in disarray in the apartment. The pillow was on the floor.

"Two guesses what that stain is on the bed sheet, Tony!"

"It's blood, Doc!"

"Nose bleed or menstruation?"

"You don't think it's either of those any more than I do."

[155]

They found Mae in the bathroom, in the tub. José officially pronounced her dead. Tony wrote the time in his notebook.

"No animal this time! Throat intact. Looks like she was choked. Purple around the throat and – oh, oh!"

"What, Doc?"

"Look here, Tony! Two puffy wounds in the side of her neck."

"The bastard makes a meal of everything he does!"

"Neater this time."

"Pretty little gal!" Tony called in the crew from headquarters and gave the location. "They ain't gonna find any, but they gotta search for prints too."

"And I can tell you the coroner isn't going to find anything but a busted neck and two tooth marls on the side of it. He'll call it death by strangulation."

"Used that smoke routine to get in and out."

"Well, we know now he's on the island in some rental unit. Using stolen money to pay cash for everything."

After the crew arrived the two men left the scene in their respective cars but planned their next move first.

"You're going to have to check all rental condos somehow."

"So what do I tell the men we're looking for? A puff of smoke? A wolf? I can't tell them we are lookin' for a coffin with a guy who gets up at night sleepin' in it! And how do I convince good old Southern Baptist rednecks they got to wear a scarf at all times while lookin'? We can't use them in our searchin'!"

"And how do I convince a judge to issue search warrants to all of you?"

"So what do we do?"

"We need bait. We got to come up with someone who's seen this thing, that bastard don't know about."

"Be pretty risky for that person!"

"This Opfer isn't a dummy! We can't use a secret person for bait."

"It's gonna have to be one of us, Doc!"

"My wife! Pam! She'll cooperate in a way that Archie wouldn't!"

"What if this German guy is one that don't like Blacks?"

[156]

"Look what happened to Annie and Joab! I'd say he's the least prejudice drinker there is."

"So what do we do? Put her on the tube spouting anti-Semitic stuff all over?"

"She wouldn't do that. She's a school teacher!"

"So come up with something!"

"We publicize that she is the one that discovered Rudy spoke German. And that she thinks the missing coffin and Licht's murder are connected and plans to check with Poland to find out who was in that coffin. We do it in a public interview on TV."

"I'll get this stuff out to the media. Make damn sure she wears that scarf all day and night, Doc, same as us."

"Good evening. Doctor White." The speaker sounded like he had a very bad case of laryngitis.

Without turning from the television set, José pulled the shawl out of the front of his shirt. "Is this a social call, Herr Opfer?" He held the shawl out in front of his chest. "Yes, I am with others that are your enemy, and I will try my best to help destroy you. No matter how long it takes, we will win!"

"Is not Opfer an interesting name? Your wife translated it for you. A very remarkable woman, your wife, for a *schvartze*."

"Much wiser than you imagine, Sir!"

"Sooner or later you will all err in my favor and I shall be ready."

José turned his head slightly in the direction of the voice but it stayed back in the shadows that covered the far side of the room.

"You mean you'll find us without these safety covers?"

"Something like that. I can wait!"

"And what if we bathe in the daytime and bask at the beach in the sunlight? And spend the rest of our time searching for you?"

"Patience! That is all I need, and I have all the time in the world to await your misstep. That will come! That will come!"

"Perhaps not. Is this a social call?"

"Sociability implies relaxation. I find it hard to do while you wear that garment you keep fingering, Doctor."

"Surely, you don't expect me to remove it to be polite?"

[157]

"You are too intelligent to do that. And we both know that while you wear it I am unable to get your direct ocular attention."

José was extremely frightened but kept his composure. "I am fully aware of your hypnotic abilities."

"Why should you be my enemy? Why do you and your band fight me?"

"What a stupid question on your part, after the horrors you've committed on our island!"

"You do not know what horror is unless you have lived in my time and breathed your last with me."

"How does this world today atone for your past misery? Not in your way!"

"That is for me to decide. In my final moments I cursed God and have received this punishment for my sins in doing so. You and your wife are my sworn enemies. You imperil my existence and I cannot allow that to continue. I have waited for over half a century fully aware that satisfaction was coming to me. I need nobody and I see nobody and I go nowhere for diversion. I have no deadlines so there is plenty of time to search for those whom I hate. When I am finished here I go to Argentina for much unfinished business. And listen to me; I shall have an entourage by then!"

"Revenge on German Nationals who've managed to evade justice so far?"

"Hear my story, Doctor White, and then decide for yourself how justified I am. My story starts before you were born." When the creature pronounced his name it was started with a 'V'.

"I was born in Frankfort. In the early years of my life, we all stayed there, together. My father had business interests in Poland and we moved to Warsaw."

"I should tell you before you go ahead with this tale that it will make no difference in my group's attitude toward you."

"Be that as it may." The creature seemed to ignore José and continued relating his autobiographical account. "My wife was a local beauty in our suburb. We produced two beautiful children, both girls. We were trapped in the Warsaw ghetto when the uprising took place there, despite being German Nationals. First

[158]

we were Jews! Twelve Nazi soldiers raped my twelve year old daughter and we were made to watch while they did this, one by one, and then they stuffed manure in her mouth and we watched her die. Our baby they swung like a rag in the air and dashed her brains out against a brick wall of the house. My wife was pulled from my arms, screaming, and I was clubbed unconscious. When I awoke I found myself in a closet in a house. My toilet was the closet floor. After what I think was maybe two or three days, the door was unlocked and I was handed a bowl of sour milk and some stale crackers."

"Then what?"

"I was handed a large box."

"Containing what?"

"My wife's head!"

"Oh, my God!"

"God? Where was God? How could he allow these things to happen? We prayed and devoted ourselves to Him; for a thousand or more years we have been his devoted children. Kept his name alive! Why does he insist on testing that faith? Like Abraham, Job! I was put on a train. In a boxcar, which, in your wildest imagination you could not endure! So crowded with humans you could not inhale for a deep breath. People screaming all the time on that trip. And then thrust inside a barn for a shower. All of us, men, women, and children, naked. I knew right away it was not a shower. Losing control of urine! Of bowels! Then from the ceiling! It burned my throat. Impossible to hold your breath; to avoid the gas! I denounced God at that moment!"

"And as a result you are what you are?"

"I suppose so! And it is my assigned duty to avenge millions of innocents. You see! Even God has blood on his hands."

"And we are committed to stop you."

"Garlic? Wolf Bane? A stake in my heart? Silver Bullets? There is no way for you to manage this. That is why I am here now. To impress the impossibility on you and your friends. You force me to strike you instead of the guilty in this world."

"You haven't listed all the ways to get at you."

"Name the others."

[159]

"Sunlight for one. God given rays will do you in, Sir. So will fire! And there are words of exorcism to be used against you. We'll manage to come up with something."

"You have wisdom beyond your years, Doctor; as does your wife. I shall meet this rabbi. I cannot allow your threats to go on. Your guard will fall and then I shall pounce."

José never saw the creature which stayed in the shadows. He turned his head toward that side of the room and beheld a large wolf with eyes that glowed as if lit from behind. José pulled the shawl out into the open and the animal disappeared. In its place was a cloud which drifted out through the crack in the door. José ran and opened the door.

"We'll get you!" he shouted to the darkness outside.

Pickett's phone rang. It was José.

"You're working late!"

"Got a crew watching cows. Phone in every so often."

"Guess with whom I've been talking! Right here in my den!"

"Shit! In person?"

"Relax! He's gone but he doesn't crave human blood."

"So I got to raise a posse and protect the herd."

"He's on a specific mission."

"Did he try and attack you?"

"I don't think so. These shawls really work. Big religious stuff involved. Didn't realize how scared I was until he left."

"How did Pam react to all of this?"

"She's at a P.T.A. meeting."

"She left it some time ago. My guys followed her to your house and then left for awhile. Take that damn scarf and see if her car is in your garage. Move!"

José slammed down the phone and ran out to the garage through the side door of the house. Her car was there but she was not.

"Oh God! No! Please! No!"

He met her as she left school. "I've been waiting for you. I want to talk with you."

"I am a bit jumpy and a good bit frightened these days. Look both ways on a one way street."

[160]

"That's understandable. Let's get in my car after you leave yours at home."

"Okay, Rabbi. Let me talk with the guards. They can go to the bathroom or whatever while we talk."

The deputies drove off after seeing her enter the rabbi's car. She intended to hear what he had to say and then go into the house and join her husband.

"We are going to the temple, Mrs. White. There is something I want to show you there."

It was right after they had driven off that José ran out to check the garage for his wife's car. He called Pickett in a state of panic.

Rabbi Silman led Pam to the rear of the temple and to the site where the shrine had been intended. "You must lure the thing to this spot, Pam. I think we can destroy it on this site."

"That is incorrect." The voice came from the shadows behind them. It was a raspy voice. "In the tomb, yes! But I do not enter such a place readily or willingly at this time."

"My husband described that voice. It's the thing!"

"Stay close behind me and finger your shawl."

"Yes. The shawl repels me! I cannot come close to it. You were wise when you discovered that, Rabbi Silman."

"You know my name?"

"My amount of knowledge would amaze you."

"We shall alert the world to this shawl."

"That would be a logistical problem, Rabbi; Insurmountable. I have been following you, Mrs. White. I shall warn you both as I have warned your husband. You will spend your days looking over your respective shoulders for me. I shall win in the end, I assure you."

"Only at night do we fear. Not in the daytime. You are a wretched victim and we are pledged to destroy you."

"Understand, Rabbi Silman. I have been cursed by the same God whom I denounced at my demise. You cannot imagine how I suffered my death. And lost whatever faith I had in Him. And now I seek revenge for what he allowed to happen to His chosen people. I go next to Argentina and then on to Poland and Germany."

[161]

"Attacking those you consider anti-Semitic?"

"It is a task he has given me."

"Listen here, buster. I'm sick of listening to you and your idiotic talk. My people also got a lot of bad sass in the past and still do in the present. Not much difference between 'kike' and 'nigger' is there? You're the bimbo who's gonna make the booboo!"

"You are my sworn enemy because you threaten me so. I will eventually eliminate you."

From where the voice had come from, they could now make out a large wolf with glowing eyes. The couple flapped their shawls and the animal howled and disappeared.

"My goodness! If my pulse slows down maybe my red cells will be able to pick up enough oxygen to let me breath more easily. I am scared! Damn, that was awful! Had close calls back in Africa when I was a kid but nothing like this."

As they drove up to the White's home, searchlights were playing around the area. Tony Pickett and José ran up to the car together.

"Where the hell have you been?"

"Close to that site," said the rabbi. He described the adventure they'd just had.

"You really shouldn't go off on your own, Pam," said Tony.

"We may spend a long time looking over our shoulders. I would hate to have to teach all day and then spend the night looking behind me and doing little else."

"You folks have really set him off now. He wants to go abroad. South America and Europe. And with an army of helpers. How do we stop him?"

"I really don't know," said the rabbi.

"He's gonna want more Rudy Singletons. Many will come from around here apparently."

"I better alert the E.R. to watch for anemics with red marks on their necks."

"Gotta be careful not to let the public in on this. Upset the tourist trade. Mayor will be on my ass."

"Not much choice is there, Tony?"

[162]

"Not much, Mrs. White. I guess the public has a right to protect itself. I don't give a damn about the commercial interests. I oughta show them all pictures of Archie. They don't like to make it too public when things happen behind the gates. Slows down sales!"

"Listen. Let's slow down! I am just an employee of the Lord. A so-called spiritual leader on salary. But I intend to tell other so-called leaders to warn their flocks about this horror."

Tony grinned. "I think them leaders are gonna laugh you out of the circle when you hand them these details. I am gonna throw this stuff at the town council. Probably get canned eventually. They ain't gonna go for science fiction."

"People have to be given the chance to defend themselves."

"So we equip the East coast with these shawls, Rabbi?"

"If possible, yes!"

"The bozo was right. We got a logistics problem," said Pam. The group parted, agreeing to wait one more day and to intensify their search during the daylight hours.

"You gave me a hell of a scare, Pam," said José to his wife after the others had left and they were back in the house. Outside, two deputies sat in a patrol car wearing scarves that the chief had insisted they keep around their necks, and thinking he was a little crazy these days.

"Bet I was closer to that wolf than you were out by that temple shrine spot."

"He was right here in the house. That's pretty close."

"Notice the eyes?"

"Hard not to."

"Think that wolf had fleas?"

The statement read to them by Tony Pickett left the members of the town council in a state of shock and disbelief.

"You been drinkin' on the job, Pickett?" asked the mayor.

"I never drank on any job. Been sober for over seven years now. I kinda expected this kind of reaction from you. You'd be quite surprised to know who else is in on this."

[163]

"You can't publish crap like this. You want to start a panic? People be leaving here in droves. We can't afford something like that."

"I felt it was some kind of 'crap' the way you do at first. But what I have seen convinces me."

"Do you expect us to swallow this shit? Turns smoke into a wolf! And vice versa! You have guts telling us that!"

"It's not shit, Sir!"

"Come on now, Chief! You want to sell scarves to everybody on the island. That's crass commercialism. Nobody will swallow nonsense like that!"

"Do we print the name of the island on the scarf?" asked another member of the council.

"Look!" Pickett pulled his shawl from under his shirt and showed it to the group.

"You gotta be a nut!"

"I assure you gentlemen that I am not crazy. Quite sane!"

"I question that. You bein' sane."

One of the members rose to his feet. "I vote against this. It's nonsense and bad publicity! Public relations would be deadly for us. We'd never live it down! The whole South would be laughing at us. Vampires, wolves, smoke figures! What the hell is this, Disneyland?"

"Pickett, I am going to call in outside help for you. Maybe the F.B.I. We got a serial killer here and you can't catch him." The mayor was angry now. "So exactly who is helping you?"

Tony named the group.

"That's it? A Jew, a Puerto Rican, and a Black? That's your roster?"

"No! A religious leader, a graduate student teacher, and a professional, a doctor."

"Now watch how you express yourself here, Pickett!"

"No! You watch! I wish I hadn't heard you just now, Mister Councilman. You ain't fit to sit there. I will see that you are quoted, word for word."

"And you ain't fit to carry a badge. This ain't a movie scenario! We got real murders here."

Another member of the council stood up and applauded.

The mayor took over. "Now fellows! Lets calm down. You got to admit, Pickett, that what you've told us sounds as if you've lost it."

"Except I seen it for myself!"

A secretary entered the room. "Phone for you, Chief."

Pickett left and picked up the phone in the outer room. "Jesus! I'm on my way!"

He returned to face the group. "Sorry, gents! Got an important lead. I'll let you know what happened as soon as I follow up on this. May take pictures so you can scare your kids." He turned and left without saying another word.

Pambazuko White, teacher of the second grade, addressed her class. The children were aged seven to nine. "Put your calculators on your desks now. We're going to see some slides." It always amazed her how children were able to grasp a bit of the concept of mathematics using pocket calculators at such an early age. Some of these children were even studying foreign languages. The level of intelligence here was much higher than that of hers at the same age. It had to do with the teaching equipment plus the family background. These kids mostly came from financially well-to-do origins.

The slide projector was at the rear of the classroom and she walked back to it.

"Now we are going to see what endangered animals look like. These are animals that are in danger of disappearing from the earth because of changes in the food and the places they live. When we build a house whoever lived on that land has to move. The forests and lands are all homes to them. Where would you live if we burned down your house? Now, who knows what this is?"

A hand shot up. "That's an eagle, Missus White!"

"That's right. They usually live in mountainous places and fly high up in the sky. They have really good eyes and can see all the way down to where they spot food. Their houses are called 'aeries.'"

"Are we moving the mountains from them, Missus White?"

[165]

"No. We build homes where they used to roost, sit, and we cut down trees and take away resting places." She flashed another slide.

"That's a cougar!" called out a child. There's a tv ad shows one jumping on a car in a park. That's the car's name too!"

"And that was an old car used to be sold here. Cougars are disappearing too."

Several voices sounded at the same time for the next slide.

"That's a wolf!"

"And they live in deep caves in deep forests. Has anybody ever seen a wolf, maybe in the zoo?"

"There's one lives across the street from me."

Pam froze. "Now, George! Not on Breakers View Island!"

"But I watch him every night when I go to bed."

"Okay, George! You stay after class is over and tell me about him, okay?"

She tried to stay calm for the rest of the day. Class was dismissed at two thirty.

"Now, George! Tell me about the wolf who lives across the street from you."

George was a short child dressed in corduroy slacks and a red shirt. He had a head of curly red hair to match his shirt.

"Well now! It really is a wolf! He goes out every night right after *Jeopardy!* That's the time I have to go to bed. Ma says next year I'll have to do some schoolwork at home after school so I can stay up later. Rather watch TV. Do you watch TV, Missus White?"

"Oh yes! Every night. I don't go out at night like your friend across the street. Where do you suppose he goes?"

"Well now, I can see his house from my bedroom. Probably chases after the *Three Little Pigs* or somebody, I guess. Isn't that what wolves do? He cooks though before he goes out and the smoke comes out through the door. I got up once real early. It was still dark and there he was coming home. At that hour! Bet Missus Wolf was mad!"

She dismissed George and ran for her cell phone in the rear closet of the room and called Tony Pickett. Then she went to the front office of the school and copied down the home address of George.

Tony drove rapidly to the White's home, arriving at the same time as José, who'd been called after Tony.

The mood was of extreme excitement. "Now let's stay calm and not get too carried away. This could be a smoke screen. Now why in the hell did I use that phrase?" Tony was quite excited.

Pam told them both of the occurrences at the school. She too, was excited and spoke very rapidly in relating what the child had told her.

"So where's he live?" asked José.

"Sandy Cove Plantation."

"Well, it's now four-thirty. We got about two hours until that program starts."

"Let's try not to involve the kid," said Tony.

"He's being cared for by a maid while the parents are away. She picks him up after school every day."

The rabbi arrived at that moment.

"Made pretty good time. Exceeded the speed limit, did you?"

"I cannot tell a lie, Officer. God and the law must forgive me! I brought what I may need."

"Me too," said José.

"We're going in the pickup truck. I hope to god this is it!" Tony drove rapidly.

The house was located on a quiet street not far from the oceanfront. It was an area with little traffic. The street was a dead-end with a large central curve as one approached the site. The nearby sound waters could be seen at a small distance to the east of the dwelling. It would be labeled "third row waterfront" in real estate advertisements. On the opposite side of the street were four condo-type dwellings. They were small and obviously created by the same architect. None seemed to be occupied. Across from the small homes were three large houses, much more luxurious in appearance. Two of these had second floors. This small group of dwellings was somewhat isolated in a newly developing area of the plantation. The nearest full development was across a golf fairway to the rear of the large homes. Trees

[167]

had been cleared for this area making it appear somewhat desolated. Small trees planted around the larger homes would take years to be effective for any shade.

The county pickup truck held four passengers. Pickett parked the vehicle in front of one of the three large homes. A brick chimney was on the left side. The garage had been built to hold three vehicles. As they walked up to the front door, they passed several lawn sculptures resembling fish. The lawn had obviously been planted with sod. One could still see the square outline of the sod pieces.

Tony rang the doorbell. It was answered by a Black domestic, wearing a white uniform dress. "Ain't nobody home! Away! Due back in two or three weeks. Call back then, please!"

"This is a police matter, Miss."

"Didn't call no police. Nothing wrong here."

"Nobody says there's something wrong. I didn't accuse you or anybody else of anything. We just want to examine the inside. Georges room."

"What that kid done now? He steal something? He's just a little kid. You gonna scare him. I ain't gonna let you in. You wait until his folks come back in a couple weeks. I'm in charge here. And I don't let nobody in. George ain't here anyhow. He's playing at his friends house. What he do? Bad in school? He act up when the folks go away."

"He didn't do anything bad. I'm his school teacher. He told us something important about his room and we want to check it out."

"He don't have nothing hidden up there I don't know about. No way I gonna let you in."

Tony took a sheet of paper from his pocket. "See this? It's a summons written by a judge. Says we got the right to look at anything we want to look at. We can arrest anybody stops us. You want me to drag you off to jail? Who's gonna look after George with you in jail?"

This frightened the poor woman. She backed up and allowed them to enter the house. She led them to a stairway leading up to the bedrooms. The stairway was located to the left side of a small alcove at the entry way next to a small closet.

"Don't think you got a right to look inside this house. Nosy around like you own it. I gonna tell George's parents 'bout you. That's George's room over there."

"Thank you. What's your name?"

"Pickney! Miz Pickney, and I never tangle with the police in my life. My family been on this island since the big war. Never caused no trouble."

"There are a lot of Pickney's on this island and all good citizens. I know your family. George says he saw something from his room and we want to check it out. That's all! This may take a while. Listen to me, Miz Pickney. Take your car and go pick up George when it's time. Take him somewhere for supper and stay away from here for at least three hours. I Promise to leave all in good order. We won't move anything and certainly won't steal anything. Copy down the number on that county truck. It's a government owned vehicle. You can report that number."

"Okay! I still think you a bunch of real estate folks trying to see what's available around here. I gonna report you to the police, besides George's folks."

"And I will leave you a note here excusing you from any responsibility for anything that happens here."

"I gonna leave like you say but I don't like it at all."

The group went into the boy's room and peered out at the condos across the street.

"It's got to be that one. It's the only one I can see from this position." Pam had lain down on the boy's bed.

"Let's go see."

Tony had been given the pass key to the villas. It was late afternoon and the sun was beginning its journey to the horizon. The door opened into a small sitting room. Beyond and to the left of this was the passageway to the kitchenette. The near end of the sitting area was also the dining area. There was a stench as if a hundred cans of tuna had been left open to dry. José opened two windows. The rabbi walked over to the wall and turned on an air conditioning switch. He then walked into the bedroom.

"He's in here!" he exclaimed in a loud whisper.

[169]

A long wooden box sat on the bed. The mattress had been pulled off and sat on the floor along side. José opened the blinds and then the windows. The odor was almost unbearable.

"Feels like I'm in at the climax of a western movie. This is it folks!" Tony opened the clasps of the box on the bed. They all pulled their shawls forward instinctively at the same moment. Tony lifted the lid as the rabbi began a chant in Hebrew. It was a text he'd had in his pocket since the Rudy singleton episode. His voice hit highs and lows as he rocked on his feet, saying the words of the exorcism. These he had found in his research of the subject of Jewish demons.

Hans Opfer lay on his back as though taking an afternoon nap. Tony lifted the right arm which was bare to the elbow.

"Somebody write this number down. Maybe the poor bastard can be identified."

There was no rose and fall of the chest as in respiration. José unrolled a small canvas kit and laid it alongside the head of Opfer. He began the beheading. This task was accomplished in about ten minutes. He laid the head between the legs. The men picked up the box and after closing it, carried it out to the truck and loaded it into the back.

They cleaned up the condo and removed a pile of men's clothing. To all intents and purposes, the condo was left as if it had never been occupied. It was as empty as the two neighboring condos on either side, across from George's home and his bedroom window.

As they left the plantation, a patrol car was just entering in response to a report of trespassing.

Tony drove to an area that they had prepared for this. It was completely isolated. A clearing in the center held three support horses on which the three men placed the box. Rabbi Silman began his chant again. The sun was setting now and, despite what was in the box, they became nervous. José poured kerosene over the body inside, particularly soaking the head. Pam handed him a sheet of paper, which Tony lit. When the paper flared up in flame, Jose threw it into the box. There was a flashing sound as the gas took flame. They stood silently for forty minutes until

[170]

all was consumed by the fire. The only sound was the rabbi's voice chanting the words of exorcism.

Pam took a small box from her jacket pocket and scooped up a small amount of the dirt and ashes. "Small souvenir of a big moment in my life!"

"I suppose we should have taken some pictures."

"You won't need any, Tony. The town fathers will be so happy that the trouble is over they won't pursue a thing. You'll see! They won't dare pass on what you told them because it would make them look too stupid to the public. Particularly if you say 'no comment.'"

"I know just what I'm gonna say to the media. We cornered the responsible party and, in a chase, he wrecked his car and was burned up. Nothing to show for the while episode."

Tony turned to Ira. "Rabbi, if it's ok with you, I am gonna keep this one more night and then burn it up."

"And I will continue to wear mine. But I will wash it much more often."

~THE FINAL VICTIM~

Epilogue

José and Pambuzuko White attended a seminar in Vienna that year. They had begun to take advantage of these medical sponsored trips which were tax deductible and also educating. They traveled about Europe after the course's end. In Warsaw, José tried to look up his old school chum, only to discover he'd been transferred, not to Latin America, but to Hawaii. Pam was beginning to show signs of her pregnancy now and they still had another week in Kenya coming up.

Out of curiosity, the Whites decided to visit Treblinka. That had been on José's mind since the beginning of the trip. After the events earlier in the year, it seemed the thing to do.

A taxi took them to that wretched site. They asked where the housing development was that had been erected over the accidently discovered mass grave.

A small row of small homes had been built in a line down the length of the site on two sides. It was almost disappointing to them. The origin of their moment of horror in history was unidentifiable. They returned to the awaiting taxi. Pam turned around.

"Be right back. Wait a second."

She returned to the row of little homes and between the last two she stooped and took a small box from her purse. She opened it and emptied the contents on the ground and then returned to the cab.

A small breeze spread the tiny amount of material she had emptied there about the area. As the taxi drove off, a small wisp of smoky vapor appeared and drifted off into the woods nearby.

~ABOUT THE AUTHOR~

I have known and been with Larry Jukofsky for over four score years now from his beginnings in New Jersey to his years at Columbia and med school and ophthalmological training in St. Louis, where he met and married Betsy. He went through part of the Korean War as the eye doctor for the First Marine Division, finally settling for a time back in practice in New Jersey. He moved to Hilton Head and has been there with Betsy for the last thirty years. He has two kids, four grandchildren, and four great grandchildren. "There's no better latitude in the world than South Carolina!"

~Other Books By Graveyard Publishing~

You can find books by Graveyard Publishing on our website. Many of our books are also available through Amazon, Barnes & Noble, and other fine book sellers. Please visit us online at:

http://www.graveyardpublishing.com/

Beginners Guide To Psychic Development
By Katrina Bowlin-MacKenzie

Ever want to take a Psychic Development class, but don't have the time, or you can't find a class nearby? The author of this book has been teaching the class for almost thirty years..
The book is written informally and starts off with learning the Tarot, to the properties of stones, The Pendulum, The Chakras, The Aura, Meditation and Healing. Included in the final chapter are daily Affirmations and how to build a Manifestation Board. In this book is all the information of a Beginners Psychic Development class, so you can learn at your own pace.

Ashes From Another Life
By: C. A. Brennan

A poetic view of the darker side of life through the eyes of a dark Sorceress. A beautiful collection of dark poetry.

In Devotion To The Crone
By: The Herban Goddess

This volume of poetry is a gift of devotion and dedication to my Goddess, the Great Crone Hecate. I offer this with humility and gratitude because I understand that the Goddess shows us each a different spectrum of light which She knows is best to reveal our truth. All that we can do in Her service is follow the light we see toward our destiny. This is the wisdom of a Crone.

[177]

Little Black Book Of Spells
By: C. A. Brennan

The Author - A Masseen Sorceress and practitioner of Dark Witchcraft for over thirty years presents this "Little Black Book Of Spells" for those who are not afraid to explore the darker aspects of their nature, and the darker aspects of their craft. A beautiful and rare collection of dark spells and writings.

Uncomfortable Silence
By Brandy Delight.

A journal of painful memories, haunting dreams, and living nightmares. Recollections from feeling lonely, without ever being alone. That awkward, uncomfortable silence... Outrage and distress of lover's lost... Torment and abuse by friends and family... Self destructive exploitation and mutilation... A woman faithless and scorned, with a longing for eternal love... A memoir of desperation found at the bottom of an empty beer bottle...

Mint Juleps, Mud Pie and MacBeth
By Bronwen Forbes

Everyone who has ever acted onstage or worked behind the scenes of a play knows that Shakespeare's shortest, bloodiest play, MacBeth, is cursed. Actors and audience members have died during performances, storms have destroyed theaters where it was playing, and even quoting famous lines from the play can bring about show-stopping disaster.

So when the tackiest, most tasteless dinner theater in the Midwest launches its own musical version of MacBeth, complete with dancing witches, an unruly dog, a Wiccan assistant stage manager and the Curse, things are bound to get interesting.

[178]

A Walk Through The Shadows
By: S. M. Brennan

The author presents this poetic journey through images of lust, violence, and darkness through the mind of a Dark Sorcerer.

Dark Hierarchy - Dark Path Powers And Spirits
By S. M. Brennan

The Author presents this listing of Dark Path Powers and Spirits as a guide book for those who walk the Dark Path, and especially for those who practice the arts of Masseen Sorcery. A comprehensive listing of Dark Path Powers and Spirits that those of the Masseen Ways, or those of other Dark Paths can call upon to aid them in their Rituals or Workings.

Incense Formulary - How To create And Blend Your Own Incenses
By S. M. Brennan

This book is a formulary and guide book for those who are interested in creating and blending their own incenses.

Masseen Sorcery - Revised Edition
By S. M. Brennan

The Author presents this Dark Arts Grimoire as an educational guide to the teachings and practices of Masseen Sorcery. Beginning with the History of Darkness and the basic knowledge and teachings of the Masseen Ways, this volume will guide the student through the Initiations, Dedications, and practices needed to work within this magickal   path.
This book includes information on basic rituals and teachings, banishments and dedications of the Masseen Path. It also includes information on sensitive's and sight,

[179]

working with mediums, spell casting, healing magick, earth magick, money spells, banishments, love magick, sex magick, color magick, destructive magick, sigils, as well as an in depth chapter on demonology, and much more. All from a Dark Path point of view.

LaVergne, TN USA
18 February 2011
217194LV00003B/95/P